THE DARLINGTON LETTERS

TRACY GRANT

COPYRIGHT

The Darlington Letters
Copyright © 2018 by Tracy Grant
Print KDP ISBN: 9781728626222
Print BN ISBN: 9781641970631
Print IS ISBN: 9781641970723

NYLA Publishing
121 W 27th St., Suite 1201, New York, NY 10001
http://www.nyliterary.com

For Suzette

ACKNOWLEDGMENTS

As always, huge thanks to my wonderful agent, Nancy Yost, for her support and insights. Thanks to Natanya Wheeler for once again working her magic to create a beautiful cover and for shepherding the book expertly through the publication process, to Sarah Younger for superlative social media support and for helping the book along through production and publication, and to Amy Rosenbaum and the entire team at Nancy Yost Literary Agency for their fabulous work. Malcolm, Mélanie, and I are all very fortunate to have their support.

Thanks to Eve Lynch for the meticulous and thoughtful copyediting and to Raphael Coffey for magical author photos.

I am very fortunate to have a wonderful group of writer friends near and far who make being a writer less solitary. Thanks to Veronica Wolff and Lauren Willig, who both understand the challenges of being a writer and a mom. To Penelope Williamson, for sharing adventures, analyzing plots, and being a wonderful honorary aunt to my daughter. To Jami Alden, Tasha Alexander, Bella Andre, Allison Brennan, Josie Brown, Isobel Carr, Catherine Deborah Coonts, Coulter, Deborah Crombie, Carol Culver/Grace, Catherine Duthie, Alexandra Elliott, J.T. Ellison,

Barbara Freethy, C.S. Harris, Candice Hern, Anne Mallory, Monica McCarty, Brenda Novak, Poppy Reifiin, Deanna Raybourn, and Jacqueline Yau.

Thank you to the readers who support Malcolm and Suzanne and their friends and provide wonderful insights on my Web site and social media.

Thanks to Gregory Paris and jim saliba for creating and updating a fabulous Web site that chronicles Malcolm and Suzanne's adventures. To Suzi Shoemake and Betty Strohecker for managing a wonderful Google+ Discussion Group for readers of the series. Thanks to my colleagues at the Merola Opera Program who help me keep my life in balance. Thanks to Peet's Coffee & Tea at The Village, Corte Madera, for welcoming me and my daughter Mélanie and giving me some of my best writing time. And thanks to Mélanie herself, for inspiring my writing, being patient with Mummy's "work time", and offering her own insights at the keyboard. This is her contribution to this story – eyhheeiftfgvfdgdcfgdgdhdyte – in Mélanie language that means, "this book was written by Tracy Grant, my mom."

DRAMATIS PERSONAE

*INDICATES REAL HISTORICAL FIGURES

The Rannoch Family & Household

Malcolm Rannoch, former Member of Parliament and British intelligence agent
Mélanie Suzanne Rannoch, his wife, former French intelligence agent
Colin Rannoch, their son
Jessica Rannoch, their daughter

Laura Fitzwalter, Marchioness of Tarrington, Colin and Jessica's former governess
Lady Emily Fitzwalter, her daughter
Raoul O'Roarke, Laura's fiancé, Mélanie's former spymaster, and Malcolm's father

Miles Addison, Malcolm's valet
Blanca Mendoza Addison, his wife, Mélanie's companion
Pedro Addison, their son
Valentin, footman

Gisèle Thirle, Malcolm's sister
Andrew Thirle, her husband
Ian Thirle, their son

The Davenport Family
Lady Cordelia Davenport
Colonel Harry Davenport, her husband, classical scholar and
former British intelligence agent
Livia Davenport, their daughter
Drusilla Davenport, their daughter

Archibald (Archie) Davenport, Harry's uncle
Lady Frances Davenport, his wife, Malcolm's aunt
Francesca Davenport, their daughter
Philip Davenport, their son
Chloe Dacre-Hammond, Frances's daughter

Aline Blackwell, Frances's daughter
Geoffrey Blackwell, her husband
Claudia Blackwell, their daughter

Others

Algernon, Lord Weston, Chancellor of the Duchy of Lancaster
Anne, Lady Darlington, his former love

Helen Trenor, Lady Marchmain, Lady Darlington's cousin
Lord Marchmain, her husband
Alexander (Sandy) Trenor, their son
Elizabeth (Bet) Simcox, his mistress

Hubert Mallinson, Earl Carfax, Malcolm's former spymaster
Amelia, Countess Carfax, his wife
Mary Laclos, their eldest daughter

Gui Laclos, her husband

Sir Hugh Cresswell
Lady Cresswell, his wife

Lord Beverston
Roger Smythe, his son
Dorinda Smythe, Roger's wife
Marina Smythe, their daughter

*Emily, Countess Cowper, patroness of Almack's

Sylvie, Lady St. Ives, French émigrée and agent

Julien St. Juste, agent for hire

There's beggary in the love that can be reckon'd.
—Shakespeare, *Antony and Cleopatra,* Act I, scene i

CHAPTER 1

London
April, 1819

ist swirled through the thick dark of the London night. Malcolm Rannoch shrank back against the rough boards of the dockside warehouse. Old instincts surfaced like hairs rising to an electric current. A spy's instincts never left him. Or was he a fool to find adventure in what was probably a perfectly commonplace outing? He could hear his wife's affectionate mockery. *You can't leave it behind any more than I can, darling.*

The river was a shadowy line, mist clinging to the water. The grease and grime so obvious by daylight blended into the shadows, but the smell choked the air, sharp and sour, worse because the night was unusually warm for April. Coal smoke, human waste, sweat, rotting slops. London. So different from standing on the shores of Lake Como. Or in the wind on the Scottish coast, the salt scent sharp in the air. But he was home. The thought, still a novelty after more than three months back from exile, washed over him, bringing a warmth and comfort he hadn't admitted to anyone. Not even his wife. Especially not his wife.

Yellow pools of lamplight glowed against the cracked cobblestones to either side of him. He had deliberately taken up this position, in a gap between two warehouses, because it was also in the shadows between the lamps. The boat had pulled up before he arrived, at the base of the stairs that led down from the terrace across from him. But they'd wait until it was a bit later, and ideally until the moon was obscured, before unloading their cargo—or letting their passengers debark.

The wind picked up, bringing the damp of the water and pushing the clouds over the moon. Malcolm moved from his hiding place to the crumbling stone terrace overlooking the river. He could make out the outline of the boat below. A dark figure detached itself from the shadows and made its way to the stairs leading to the terrace, moving with an economy that somehow made it blend into the night.

Malcolm felt himself smile. Tempting to run down the stairs, but probably foolish given the company in which Raoul O'Roarke had slipped back into Britain. Malcolm melted back towards the gap between the buildings on the far side of the terrace where he had sheltered before. Less than half a minute later, Raoul appeared at the top of the stairs. Malcolm took a step out of the shadows, just as three figures from the right hurled themselves on O'Roarke.

Raoul whirled round, knocked one of the men backwards, and kicked a second even as the third jumped on his back. Malcolm ran forwards, grabbed the two on the ground by their shoulders as they scrambled to their feet, and knocked their heads together. Raoul had shaken off the third man. As Malcolm turned round, the man launched a blow at Raoul's jaw. Raoul caught the man's wrist and used his momentum to hurl him to the pavement.

Of one accord, Malcolm and Raoul ran through the alley where Malcolm had been concealed, darted into a dockside tavern, slipped through the crowd of sailors and dockworkers and women with bright hair and overly rouged cheeks, lost themselves long enough to order pints, slap down coins, and swallow a third of the contents, then went out a back door into another alley, round the corner, across two more streets, and at last paused in the doorway of a shuttered used-clothes dealer, both breathing hard. "Damn it, O'Roarke," Malcolm said, "you can't get yourself killed. You're getting married in a week."

Raoul gave the sort of grin with which he'd been defying danger for as long as Malcolm could remember. "And I have every intention of being at my wedding."

"Laura's the calmest bride-to-be imaginable, but she'll never forgive me if anything happens to you."

For a moment, in Raoul's gaze Malcolm saw the unreality of the situation. Raoul was a man who had lived his life not believing in happy endings, at least not for himself. He lived in the murky world of a spy, devoted to causes he believed would make the world a better place, but with little time to focus on himself. And the choices he'd made in the service of that cause made him unsure he deserved happiness. Malcolm understood, because he was a bit like that himself. More than a bit. After all, Raoul O'Roarke was his father.

But Raoul, recently divorced from his estranged wife, was about to marry Laura Tarrington, the woman he loved far more than he'd probably ever let himself put into words. And Laura was about to have their child. A positively domestic outcome. Save that O'Roarke, leaning against the cracked boards, a scratch on his cheek and a bruise beginning to form round his eye, didn't look in the least domestic.

"How is she?" Raoul asked. "I can never be sure she's putting the truth in her letters."

"Glowing. Telling everyone who fusses that's she's not ill, she's having a baby." Malcolm pushed his hair out of his eyes. "And no, there's no sign she's going to have the child before the wedding."

Relief shot through Raoul's gaze. Much as he, like Malcolm, might fight against the rules of society, in the world in which they lived, legal legitimacy mattered. Of course, Malcolm himself was illegitimate, but he had all the advantages of legally having been born within a marriage, which was all that counted, however many people knew to the contrary.

"What are you doing here, Malcolm?" Raoul asked.

"Meeting you. Rupert told us you were coming in tonight. What happened to Bertrand and the friend you were helping out of Spain?" Their friend Bertrand Laclos helped Bonapartists escape the reprisals of the restored Bourbon regimes in France and Spain.

"We let them off outside London without incident. I stayed on the boat to get home faster. Not that I'm not delighted to see you, but what made you anticipate trouble?"

"You're slipping into London. Need you ask more?"

"My dear Malcolm. I've been slipping in and out of London since before you were born. Including when I was a wanted man."

Malcolm stared at his father in the shifting light of the moon. After all this time, Raoul could still surprise him. "You came into London after the Irish Uprising? When there was still a warrant for your arrest?"

"You don't really think I'd have gone a year without seeing you, do you?"

Malcolm studied the man who had been there for him since his birth in ways he was only beginning to understand. Or at least to consciously acknowledge. "No. I don't think so. Not now. You never did go that long. But the risk—"

"Life's a risk." Raoul touched his arm. "I'm distinctly grateful for your help tonight. I don't know that I could have managed three on my own. But I think they were just rival smugglers. Or possibly Preventive Waterguard men, though then I think they'd have announced themselves."

"Maybe. That is, maybe they were rival smugglers."

Raoul's hand tightened on his arm. "You worry too much, Malcolm. Let's go home."

~

MALCOLM'S WIFE ANSWERED THE DOOR IN BERKELEY SQUARE. Another change since he and Mélanie had returned to Britain. They had their full staff back, but at a certain point in the evening they now sent everyone to bed and answered the door themselves. When they returned home from late nights, they used a key. Unheard of, in Mayfair.

Mélanie's gaze darted over Raoul with relief. She gave him a quick hug, then drew back and looked from him to Malcolm, taking in the bruises on their faces and the dust on their coats. "You had trouble."

"Just a brush with a few men from a rival gang," Raoul said. "Smugglers are undeniably useful, but have their challenges as traveling companions."

Mélanie slid her arm round Malcolm and pressed her head against his shoulder.

"I've only been gone a matter of hours," he said, his lips against her walnut-brown ringlets .

"I'm still relieved to have you back in one piece." She looked at Raoul. "You have a visitor. I wasn't sure—but your being here isn't secret. And it seemed important. When he learned we were expecting you tonight, he said he wanted to wait. It's Lord Weston. He's in the library."

Malcolm frowned. Weston was Chancellor of the Duchy of Lancaster, a respected Tory politician. A decent man, but not someone he'd have expected to find connected to Raoul, an avowed Radical who had worked against the British government in France, Spain, and Ireland.

Raoul's brows drew together, but he nodded without the surprise Malcolm would have expected. "I should talk to him."

They moved into the hall. Laura appeared in the library doorway as they crossed the black and white marble tiles. Raoul's gaze lightened. He went to her side, kissed her, and held her against him for a moment. "Children well?"

"Emily's asleep. And the baby as well, I think." She put her hand on her stomach. "No kicks at present."

Raoul put his hand over her own where it rested on her stomach for a moment. Laura's gaze flickered over his face. She reached up with her free hand to touch the bruise forming round his eye, a question in her gaze.

"Just a bit of excitement at the docks." He took her hand, laced his fingers through her own, and stepped into the library, drawing her with him.

Weston had been sitting in one of the Queen Anne chairs by the fire, but he stood as Raoul moved into the room. He was a tall man whose fair hair showed a touch of gray in the candlelight. Probably a few years younger than Raoul, who was one-and-fifty. To Malcolm's surprise, as he observed the scene standing behind Raoul and Laura, Raoul's and Weston's gazes met in a moment of recognition.

"I'm sorry," Weston said. "I wouldn't have disturbed you. But as I explained to Mrs. Rannoch and Lady Tarrington, this is rather urgent."

Raoul nodded, as though it was perfectly natural for a member of the British establishment to need to see an avowed revolutionary who had just slipped back into the country. "No need to apologize for calling on an old friend."

"Is that what we are?" Weston gave a wintry smile.

"It's what we were. I don't know that anything's changed." Raoul advanced into the room, drawing Laura with him. "Anything you have to say to me you can say in front of everyone here. Laura is my wife to all intents and purposes and soon will be so legally. Mélanie is Malcolm's wife. And Malcolm's my son."

Again, to Malcolm's surprise, Weston smiled. "I always thought so. Though I wasn't sure you'd ever admit it."

"A number of things have changed. If you need my help, you're going to need all of them."

Mélanie squeezed Malcolm's arm, a warning to be quiet and let the scene play out. Which he had every intention of doing, despite his curiosity. Or because of it.

Raoul and Laura moved to the sofa. Raoul helped Laura sit, keeping a protective hand on her arm as she lowered her eight-months-pregnant self, then eased down himself to the sofa with, Malcolm noted, the well-disguised care of one whose bones ached. Mélanie poured coffee from the silver pot on the sofa table, gave cups to Raoul and Malcolm, refilled Laura's, Weston's, and her own.

Weston turned his cup in his hand. "It's been a long time."

Raoul took a sip of coffee. "We don't precisely move in the same circles any longer." He looked from Laura to Malcolm and Mélanie. "Lord Weston and I knew each other many years ago, in Ireland."

Malcolm stared at the Tory politician. He'd have thought Weston would have opposed Raoul in Ireland save for the obvious friendship between the men. "You were one of the United Irishmen?"

Weston drew in and released his breath. "Not officially. But yes, I worked with them."

It was a shocking admission from one of Britain's senior politicians. An admission that could end his career. But then, Raoul already knew and could tell any of the people in this room.

"I nearly turned myself in when it all fell apart," Weston said. "It seemed I should share my comrades' fate. O'Roarke was the one who persuaded me not to."

Raoul leaned back on the sofa, his arm round Laura. "I saw no reason for you to needlessly throw your life away. There was a great deal you could make of it."

"I don't imagine you approve of what I have made of it."

"I'd hardly blame anyone for following their conscience, though I might not agree with where it took them. And in your case, I assume it *was* conscience."

Weston's fingers tightened on the handle of his cup. "Our ideas were dangerous."

"If you mean by that that they might change the world if put into practice, I trust to God they would."

Weston gave a faint smile. "You're still a madman."

"Hardly."

"Yes." Laura squeezed Raoul's fingers. "And I love you for it."

"From the look of it, you had adventures only tonight," Weston said.

"A minor skirmish," Raoul said. "Nothing like Ireland."

Weston turned to Malcolm. "I expect you're shocked."

"In this family? You can't expect me to be shocked by anyone's being a spy."

"It could ruin me. That goes without saying. One could argue that I deserve it—"

"Please let's not talk of what anyone deserves," Raoul said. "I'd come out worse than anyone in this room. What you deserve is to live the life you've built for yourself. And someone's trying to blackmail you?"

Weston's brows snapped together. "How did you guess?"

"Something sent you to seek me out now. Something brought up the past. And you were so quick to share it, I suspect you knew you'd have to do so the moment you called on us."

Weston gave a sigh that seemed to weigh his shoulders beneath the glossy fabric of his coat. "I received a blackmail letter."

"Do they have proof?" Raoul asked in a level voice.

Weston nodded. "Letters. I wrote to Anne that year." He looked at the others. "Anne Somercote. Lady Darlington now. We were—in '98 we hoped to marry one day. I didn't guard my tongue when I wrote to her."

"And she kept the letters," Raoul said.

"She says she had them in a safe place. In a compartment in her dressing table. They disappeared a fortnight ago. She told me at once." He looked among them. "You investigate things. I thought—"

"Yes," Raoul said. "You were right to come to us. And I was right to think we'd need Malcolm and Mélanie and Laura. The Rannochs are the real investigators. Though Laura and I aren't bad at it."

"Spare us the protestations, O'Roarke." Malcolm said. "Did Lady Darlington say who had access to her room, Lord Weston?"

Weston turned his coffee cup on the saucer, knuckles white as he gripped the gilded handle. "She gave a ball the night before she discovered they were missing. She can't be sure, but that seems the likeliest time."

"What do the blackmailers want?" Raoul asked.

"My resignation."

Malcolm drew a sharp breath. "Do you have any idea who they are?"

Weston shook his head. "Of course anyone in a position of power has enemies. But I always thought myself one of the duller sorts of government type. I never thought to find myself the target of a plot." He stared at his hands, then raised his gaze to Raoul. "I'm responsible for my past. One could make a case that I should own it—"

"It would curtail what you can do now."

"Which you might think is a very good thing."

"I don't think it's a good thing for anyone to be silenced, whatever their ideas."

Weston held his gaze. "You've already paid for Ireland. And the past puts you at risk again as well."

"Not so much as you, as it happens." Raoul took another sip of coffee. "I've—rather remarkably—received a pardon from the prince regent."

Weston's eyes widened.

"You didn't know?" Raoul said.

"No. But I'm hardly in intelligence circles. All the more reason to credit your investigative work."

"It was unexpected. But it may put me in a good position to help you."

"All of us," Malcolm said. "Do you have the blackmail letter? It might help us narrow things down."

Weston gave a curt nod and reached into his pocket. He drew out a plain sheet of heavy paper, the shade of table linens at Mayfair parties.

Weston,

If you don't wish your letters to the present Lady Darlington, and your actions in Ireland twenty years ago, to come to light, you will resign your position at once. We can give you until Thursday next."

Malcolm glanced at Raoul. "Do you recognize the hand?"

"No, but it may mean something to Archie."

"We'll also need a list of the guests at Lady Darlington's ball," Mélanie said.

Weston's gaze widened, in a way Malcolm had seen the gazes of many members of the beau monde do at the realization that their own were going to have to be questioned. But he nodded. "I'll talk to her. But perhaps it would be best if you called on her, Mrs. Rannoch. She might be more comfortable talking to another woman."

"We don't have the entrée in London society that we once did," Mélanie said. "We've been living more quietly since our return from the Continent."

"And Raoul's and my scandal has rather cast a pall over the family's social position," Laura said. Her voiced was composed but Malcolm caught the concern underneath.

"Thank God for it," he said with a grin. "It's a relief not to be dining out every night of the week. I'm not sure I'd have consented to return to London society otherwise."

"But we still have a number of connections," Mélanie said. "We can make inquiries. We'll do everything in our power to get the papers back. I beg you, Lord Weston, don't give way to blackmail. For your own sake and for the sake of others. It will only embolden the blackmailers to go further, and others will be hurt."

Weston inclined his head. "I take your point, Mrs. Rannoch. I acknowledge my sins, but I have no desire to put my family through scandal. I lost my wife two years ago, but our daughters are on the verge of society. They would find my disgrace difficult. And I confess I have no wish to leave my position. However, if the news becomes public, I will have to leave it regardless."

"We all know something about secrets," Mélanie said. "They're currency in the life of a spy. But secrets can be protected more often than you'd think. Give us time."

"Time is what I don't have, Mrs. Rannoch."

"We'll use it wisely," Malcolm said.

"I know how damnable waiting is," Raoul said. "Believe me, I loathe it myself. But right now, waiting is what you need to do."

Weston nodded again. "Point taken." He got to his feet. "Thank you. All of you."

Raoul stood and held out his hand. "It's good to see you again."

"You as well." Weston clasped his hand and regarded him for a long moment. "I know I've changed. I hope you'll take it as a compliment when I say I also find you quite transformed."

"I'm still the man I was. But my life has taken some fortunate turns."

Weston looked from Raoul to Laura. "My felicitations to you both."

"Thank you," Laura said. "We're very fortunate. In a number of ways."

Weston smiled. "Happiness is to be savored. I'm more aware of that than ever, these days." He regarded Raoul for another moment. "I imagine as a husband and father you'll moderate the risks you run."

Raoul dropped an arm round Laura's shoulders. "Meaning a spy shouldn't have a family? I've said so myself. I've said so to Laura. I'm very aware of the potential consequences of the risks I run these days. But, as I said, I'm still the man I was."

Weston's gaze flickered over Raoul's face. "Go carefully, my friend. You have a great deal to lose."

Raoul's arm tightened round Laura. "I'm very much aware of it."

CHAPTER 2

*M*élanie took a sip of coffee. Quiet had descended over the library when Malcolm left to see Weston from the house. Raoul had got to his feet to say goodbye to his friend and was still standing, frowning at a glass-fronted bookcase, as though the gilded book spines held answers that were tantalizingly out of reach. Laura watched him with concern for a moment, then met Mélanie's gaze. Mélanie saw the relief in her friend's eyes. Relief at having him safely back. And perhaps at having something to investigate. Mélanie felt both herself.

Malcolm came back into the room, closed the door, and turned to Raoul. "Your friends never fail to surprise me."

Raoul turned from the bookcase. "We certainly went in different directions. But he's a decent man. I hate to see the past used against him."

Malcolm gave a faint smile. "You're a fraud, O'Roarke."

Raoul raised a brow. "Of all the names I've been called in my varied career, I think that's a new one."

"For years you claimed to put the cause before all else."

In the candlelight, Mélanie thought Raoul colored slightly.

"Weston and I may disagree politically, but helping him or not hardly aids or hinders any cause of mine."

"Precisely. It's a personal choice." Malcolm returned to the settee beside Mélanie. "I hate to see his past used against him too. I hate to see that done to anyone." He leaned forwards to refill the coffee cups. "Blackmail can't but make me think of the Elsinore League."

Raoul shot a look at him. The Elsinore League were the shadowy organization begun by Malcolm's putative father, the late Alistair Rannoch. Malcolm's mother, Arabella, had fought the League for years, along with Raoul, and recently Malcolm and Mélanie had been drawn into the fight. "There's no reason to think Weston's a target of the League's. But—yes. My thoughts went there as well."

"We should look into what Weston's working on at present." Mélanie said. She took a sip of coffee, sifting through pieces of information filed away at the back of her mind from the days when all too much of her life had been taken up with the minutia of the beau monde. Fragments of conversations exchanged over teacups, across carriages in Rotten Row, in the ladies' retiring room at a ball. "Isn't Lady Darlington connected to Lady Marchmain?"

"Good God." Malcolm set down the coffeepot. "Yes, I think they're cousins."

Lord Marchmain was a powerful nobleman on the fringe of Tory politics. None of them was much connected with the family, but three months ago the Marchmains' elder son, Matthew Trenor, had proved guilty of the murder of a young woman named Miranda Dormer and also of selling foreign office secrets to the Elsinore League. Despite his father's influence, he had been deported to Australia—more, they all suspected, because of the treason than because of smothering a young woman who had worked in a brothel.

"We never connected Marchmain to the League," Malcolm

said. "He isn't on the list of members we have, and though Matthew Trenor was selling information to Beverston, Matthew didn't seem to know Beverston was part of the League or even know the League existed."

"But he might have told Beverston that Lady Darlington had once been involved with Weston," Raoul said.

"That wouldn't have meant anything to Beverston if he didn't know Weston had worked with the United Irishmen," Laura pointed out.

"No, but it might have started Beverston looking into Lady Darlington if he wanted a hold on Weston," Raoul said. "If he had someone search her things, that would have led the League to the papers."

"Or perhaps Matt Trenor even found the papers and told Beverston about them," Mélanie said. "Given his other actions, I doubt he'd have caviled at turning on his mother's cousin. Although that doesn't account for why the League waited three months to take the papers and make use of the information."

"The League often bide their time," Malcolm said. "Perhaps whatever's making them move against Weston didn't become pertinent until now. In any case, it's a connection we should pursue. I'll talk to Sandy."

Alexander Trenor, Mathew Trenor's younger brother, had become a friend in the course of the investigation three months ago, despite his brother's downfall, or perhaps at least in part because of it, as Matt's exposure had also saved the girl Sandy loved.

Malcolm looked at Raoul. "I'll try to be discreet. But I may need to trust Sandy with some of Weston's story."

Raoul nodded. "Young Trenor struck me as quite sensible beneath the naiveté. More to the point, as a fundamentally decent human being."

Malcolm nodded but continued watching Raoul. "Speaking of the League, I don't like that fight you were in tonight."

"As I told you, that was a side effect of needing to work with smugglers."

"And, as I told you, maybe it was."

"You've said often enough you're wary of coincidence," Laura reminded Raoul.

"So I am. But being attacked when one gets off a smugglers' boat is hardly coincidental."

"But suspicious when a group like the Elsinore League are trying to kill one," Malcolm said.

"They were trying to kill me eight months ago." Raoul said. They'd been in Italy when they'd uncovered that information. "They haven't been doing a very good job of it."

"As I said, the League often bide their time." Malcolm set down his coffee cup. "For God's sake, Father, be careful."

Malcolm called Raoul "Father" rarely enough that the word hung in the air, creating an island of stillness. Raoul's gaze locked on Malcolm's own. "I always am." The words might have been a deflection, but the look in his eyes was not. "Now, more than ever. For any number of reasons." His arm tightened round Laura. "But if we go into hiding, we let the League win. And none of us wants to do that."

RAOUL LOOKED OVER HIS SHOULDER AS HE CLOSED THE DOOR TO the night nursery. "Remember, it's our secret," he said before he pulled the door to.

"Colin?" Laura asked.

Raoul smiled. "He woke up when I went in, but he promises he won't tell Emily he saw me first. I swear they've both grown since I last saw them."

"You haven't been gone that long. Though they are both eating rather ferociously. Wait until you see Emily in her dress for the wedding. She looks very grown up."

He gave a bemused smile. "It's hard to credit."

"How fast the children grow?"

"That too. I meant having a family." He shrugged out of his coat. "I think Weston was shocked at the changes in me."

Laura watched her lover for a moment. As well as she knew him, there was still much of his past she didn't know. "You haven't seen him for a number of years."

"True enough. But the changes are more recent." He set the coat over a chair back. "I'm surprised at them myself."

Laura turned and stepped into his arms. "Sometimes I can still hardly believe it's real."

"Us?" He brushed his lips across her forehead. "We may not either of us be much for conventional phrases, but I thought what we felt for each other was a fairly open secret."

"Mmm." She pressed her head against his shoulder. "I had begun to have a glimmering. I didn't mean that; I meant getting married."

He lifted his head to look down at her, and in his gaze she saw something of the same wonder. It had seemed out of reach for so long. Something they had to make their relationship work despite not being able to have. "It's not anything —"

"You ever thought to find yourself doing. Again?"

"That's not what I—"

"I know. You never expected a happy ending. Not for yourself. I didn't either. Not for years. Not ever, I think."

He took her face between his hands. "Marriage is anything but an ending. Not that I really believe in endings, in any case. Not while one has life and breath."

"Nor do I. But I do believe in happiness, which I didn't for a long time. I don't think I thought I deserved it."

"That's nonsense, sweetheart."

She kissed him. "Says one guilty of precisely the same thing." And he was letting himself reach for it because he thought she deserved it. She still wasn't sure he thought he deserved happiness himself.

"If you mean I have far more good fortune than I deserve, then you're entirely right, my darling."

She drew back a little, her hands against his chest. "I once said I never wanted to marry again. That's not true anymore."

He smiled. "I'm exceedingly relieved to hear it." He put his hands over her own. "I told you if I'd been free I'd have asked you that first night in Maidstone, for all I should have given you time."

"Yes. I know. It sounded very gallant. I think you were trying to reassure me that you hadn't rushed into anything because of the baby."

"No. That is, of course I wanted to reassure you if you were so uncharacteristically foolish as to have any doubts on the matter. But I was quite in earnest. I don't know that it speaks well of me. You needed time. Because of my own situation I managed to give it to you—"

"Rather too much of it. You were halfway to running off so I'd marry someone sensible—"

"You'd be bored to tears by someone sensible."

"My point precisely."

"But I knew what I wanted. If I'd been free I don't think I'd have been able to stop myself from asking you."\

She searched his face. The sharp cheekbones, the hooded eyes, the flexible mouth. So familiar now, but at times still inscrutable. "I never thought—I didn't doubt your feelings—"

"Ha." It was his turn to laugh. "You thought I had a mistress of four-and-twenty."

"Lisette is lovely and brilliant, and we'd only made the most oblique promises to each other. It's the sort of qualm new lovers have. But though I didn't doubt your feelings, I don't think I realized how much marriage meant to you."

"I don't know that marriage does." He twined his fingers round her own. "Not in the moral sense. Not because of the eye of soci-

ety. We don't need to be married to know what
other. I may be unconventional. I may not think :
terms of marriage—"

"Nor do I." Laura recalled a conversation with Mary ᴗᴗᴗᴗᴗ,
the shore of Lake Como. "So if it wasn't for the baby—"

"But I like the idea of the commitment being public. Making it
in front of our friends and family."

She smiled at him. "That's rather lovely."

"You have a way of bringing out sentiment in me, beloved."

"Hmm. I think I just have a way of getting you to say things
you'd normally keep to yourself."

He stooped his head and kissed her. "If you'd been a British
agent you'd have been my downfall. I remember worrying about it
when I left one of our visits at Newgate."

That was how their relationship had begun. His interrogating
her while she was imprisoned in Newgate on charges of murder.
"That I was a British agent?"

"No, though perhaps I should have done. How well you could
see past defenses I took as second nature."

"Your insights terrified me. At the same time, it was such a
relief to talk to you. It was so long since anyone had seen me as
myself."

"Precisely."

She put her hands on his chest. "I want you there. When the
baby's born. I mean, beside me in the room. Do you mind?"

"How could I mind?"

"Some men would go pale at the thought. Even men who've
faced the dangers you have."

He gave a quick grin. "Oh, I didn't say I wasn't terrified. But I'm
also beyond relieved you want me there. I'd feel distinctly foolish
waiting for news anywhere else while my lover—my wife—gave
birth to our child."

Laura leaned in to him. It was remarkable that they had got to
the point they were at now. And being about to get married was

least of it. She drew a breath, drinking in the scent of his skin, he warmth of his arms, the beat of his pulse beneath her ear. Savoring the moment. Because sometimes, even now, she couldn't shake the fear that the more settled their happiness became, the greater the risk it would melt away.

~

COLIN RANNOCH OPENED HIS EYES AS MALCOLM BENT TO TUCK THE covers round him. "Uncle Raoul's back."

"Just so." Malcolm smoothed his son's hair. "Did you see him?"

Colin rolled onto his back. "I woke up when he came into the nursery. I promised I wouldn't wake Emily up or tell her tomorrow that I saw him first. After all, he's *her* father."

"So he is." Mélanie moved to her son's side. Emily had been born before Raoul and Laura met, but Colin understood that it took more than birth to make a parent. A knowledge that always brought a lump to Mélanie's throat, given her son's own tangled parentage. A complicated history they had just recently related to him, in terms as simple as possible. Colin was grappling with it, amazingly well so far, it seemed.

Mélanie looked at her husband and son for a moment, the tangle of brown hair that fell over both foreheads, the gray eyes, the flexible mouths. Malcolm had taken his coat off. The white of his shirt blended with Colin's nightshirt as he bent over the bed.

"Of course, Uncle Raoul's sort of my father too," Colin added with the matter-of-factness of almost six.

Mélanie sucked in her breath and tried to control the sound.

"Uncle Raoul's whatever you want him to be," Malcolm said in easy tones. "We told you that when we told you about your birth. He loves you very much. It doesn't change what you and I are to each other."

"But he's the only father Emily has. That makes it special. And he's your father. I like thinking of him as my grandfather." Colin frowned in consideration of a new idea. "When Uncle Raoul marries Laura, will she be my grandmother?"

"Technically your step-grandmother, scamp." Malcolm tousled his son's hair. "But I imagine she'd much prefer that you go on calling her Laura."

"That's good. I don't think I could get used to anything else. Just like Uncle Raoul said I could go on calling him Uncle. And I don't suppose she'd want you to call her Mama, either. I mean, you're the same age."

"Quite," Malcolm said.

Colin grinned. "What we call each other doesn't really matter."

Mélanie sat on the edge of the bed opposite Malcolm. "Precisely," she said. Though she knew, or could guess, what it meant to Raoul when Malcolm called him Father.

"And I don't think I could think of Emily as my aunt," Colin added, glancing across to the other bed where Emily was curled on her side, her stuffed rabbit tucked in her arm, her red-blonde hair falling over her face in a soft tangle.

"I doubt Emily could see it that way either," Malcolm said.

"Anyway, we're all a family. That's what matters." Colin turned his head on the pillow to look at Mélanie. "I'm glad Uncle Raoul's back. I'm glad he's all right."

"O'Roarke can take very good care of himself," Malcolm said.

"You always say that, but you always worry," Colin said. "He'll be here until after the baby's born now, won't he?"

"And for a bit after," Mélanie said.

"That's good. Not that London's so safe. I mean, someone attacked him tonight, didn't they?"

"Did he say so?" Mélanie asked. They all tried to be scrupulously honest with the children, but that surprised her.

"Of course not. But he had a scrape on his cheek and a bruise round his eye."

"There was a bit of trouble at the docks," Malcolm said. "Nothing serious."

"You were there?"

"I met him."

"That's good. I mean, it's always safer to have backup, isn't it?"

"Whenever possible," Malcolm agreed.

Mélanie bent to kiss their son. "Do you think you can go back to sleep?"

"I should think so. Lots to look forward to tomorrow." Colin yawned and settled back into the pillows. Mélanie pulled the covers up about his shoulders and gave a pat to Berowne, the cat, who was curled up at the foot of the bed. By the time she and Malcolm got to their feet, Colin's eyes had drifted closed.

Malcolm took her hand and they stepped into their bedchamber. "How long do you think until he starts asking to help with investigations?" she said.

"Asking?" Malcolm grinned as he pulled the night nursery door to. "I suspect he'll jump in without asking and start looking for information on his own. Or with Emily."

Mélanie went to the cradle and adjusted the blanket over two-and-a-half-year-old Jessica. "Wasn't he just learning to walk and mastering his first words?"

"It seems that way." Malcolm was unwinding his neckcloth. "Then I remember all the ways we've changed in the years since."

Six years in June since Colin's birth. Seven years in December since their marriage. Years in which they had navigated the dangers of the Peninsular War and the intrigues of the Congress of Vienna and faced the horrors of the battle of Waterloo, all the time spying for opposite sides. Years in which they had somehow managed to fall in love. In which they had both stopped spying (as much as any spy ever did), had attempted to put down roots, had a second child, settled into a life in the beau monde as they worked to build Malcolm's political career. Only to see it all almost fall to pieces when Malcolm learned the truth of her past and her reasons for marrying him. And somehow from that wreckage they had pieced their marriage back together, survived exile, returned to Britain where they were attempting to rebuild their lives. "Perhaps most of all in the last year and a half."

"Perhaps." Malcolm dropped the cravat in the laundry basket. "But I don't know that we'd have got through the last year and a half if we'd still been the people we were when we married."

Difficult to remember back to the woman she'd been when she'd married Malcolm. Focused on her cause, ruthless, as blind to a large extent to the feelings of those about her as she was to her own. Mélanie smoothed the white and silver blanket over Jessica one more time and glanced at the door to the night nursery. "Sometimes I still wonder if we were right to tell Colin."

Malcolm's gaze caught and held her own across the room. "We had to, sweetheart. There was too much risk of someone else putting the pieces together and telling him first. Besides, it's an open secret in the family that Raoul's my father. It would have been worse for Colin to learn Raoul was his grandfather and then a few years later learn he's his biological father. And he'd have known there were years of our lying to him."

"I know." It was what they'd all discussed, she and Malcolm and Raoul, before they'd talked to Colin. Malcolm had been the most sanguine, but it had been plain to all of them there was no other option.

When Mélanie had been a spy for the Bonapartist French, Raoul had been her spymaster. For part of that time, before her marriage, he'd been her lover. When she'd married Malcolm in Lisbon six and a half years ago, she'd been on a mission to extract information about British plans. A mission Raoul had agreed with. He had also, she now realized, seen the marriage as a way to keep her and the child she was carrying out of danger. That was how they had put it to Colin. That with the war and danger she and Raoul couldn't be together, that Malcolm wanted to be Colin's father, that Malcolm had loved Colin since before he was born. Colin hadn't asked questions. At least not yet. When he did, they were going to have to navigate those waters one step at a time.

Mélanie went to her dressing table and unfastened her garnet pendant. "And then, just in case we thought things were going to get too tame, Lord Weston appeared on our doorstep this evening."

"Tame?" Malcolm laughed. "With the League a threat, O'Roarke's getting attacked all too often, and everything else we're facing?"

She set the necklace in its velvet box on her dressing table. "No, but you have to admit since we returned to London we've been a bit more domesticated."

Malcolm moved to her side and set his hands on her shoulders. "What exactly are you thinking of, my darling? When you went to St. Giles last week to see a former fellow agent? When we took the children with us to Dover to help smuggle one of your comrades into the country one step ahead of Royalist agents? When I helped O'Roarke take on three ruffians tonight? If anyone's being domesticated it's O'Roarke and Laura. And they really aren't. Any more than they were a day or week or a few months ago. They're just getting married. Marriage doesn't always change things."

"It did for us."

He tucked a strand of hair behind her ear. "But then, we didn't know each other when we married."

"Funny," Mélanie said.

He raised a brow.

"Society says a woman should be married if she has a child. That's why you married me."

"That's not—"

"You'd never have risked marriage otherwise. You've said it often enough. And without that, you'd never have known me well enough to love me."

He stroked the backs of his fingers against her cheek. "I was already half in love with you when I proposed, but yes, all right."

"And here Raoul and Laura are marrying just before their child is born. But they very nearly faced having the baby and not being able to marry."

"They'd have been fine," Malcolm said. "But it will be better for the child this way. And it matters to them, I think, being able to make a formal commitment. It mattered to me."

Mélanie regarded her husband for a moment, thinking back to that day, the close air in the sitting room of the British embassy, the pressure of her mother's comb holding her mantilla in her hair, the strange rhythms of English all round her. "It didn't matter to me when we married," she said. "It does now."

Malcolm smiled. "Far better than the other way round." He pressed a kiss to her forehead.

She leaned her head against his shoulder. "Who do you think the men were who attacked you and Raoul tonight?"

"I'm not sure. They were good fighters but didn't have particular finesse. They could have been rival smugglers, as O'Roarke says. Or they could have been hired to lie in wait for him. Despite their quiet recently, I'm not convinced the League have abandoned their efforts to kill him. Though it's hard to think anyone who knows Raoul would think tonight's sort of attack would work."

"They didn't know you'd be there."

"Which is precisely why I didn't want him coming into London alone. Though most likely he could have dispatched them perfectly well on his own. If it was the League, it's more likely it was meant as some sort of warning."

"If they're behind the blackmail of Weston, they must know Weston and Raoul were friends. I can't tie it to the attack unless they really thought they could put Raoul out of commission. Or wanted him distracted."

"They might guess Weston would come to us, but not invariably. It took a fair amount of courage for him to admit the truth to his political enemies.

Mélanie realized they had gone from talking about their

marriage to talking about the threats to Raoul with scarcely a pause or hitch. The lack of undertones to the conversation was the most surprising thing about it. She glanced towards the night nursery where Colin was asleep. Colin who was Malcolm's son in every way that mattered, but who biologically was Raoul's child. A year and a half ago, when Malcolm first learned the truth, Mélanie hadn't been sure their marriage would last. Let alone that they'd ever be on good terms with Raoul. Even as things got better than she'd ever imagined, there were still moments she'd felt she was walking on eggshells. Somehow, in the chaos of leaving Britain because of her past and then of their unexpected return, they had got to the point where they not only were all friends—family—but the past no longer overshadowed the present. At least, not most of the time.

"It's difficult to know without knowing who is behind the blackmail," she said. "Or why they want to get rid of Weston."

Malcolm frowned.

"What?" Mélanie asked.

"Weston seems like a decent man. I liked him. O'Roarke likes him, which counts for a lot."

"But?" Mélanie said as her husband trailed into silence.

"I suppose a part of me is inclined to suspect someone who changes that much."

"People change. You and I have, as you just pointed out. Raoul has himself."

"Yes, but none of us changed in our essential beliefs."

"Perhaps Weston's beliefs never were as strong."

"Perhaps. Though it's hard to imagine someone taking the risk of working with the United Irishmen without fairly strong beliefs. I suspect O'Roarke would say if we're to have a prayer of success with any of the things we want to accomplish we have to be able to persuade people to our way of thinking, so we have to accept it can work the other way as well. Still—"

"It's odd," Mélanie said, studying the conflict in her husband's gaze.

"Weston's change of views?"

"That too. But I meant your suspecting someone's motives while Raoul takes the other person at face value."

Malcolm gave a twisted smile. "Yes, well, O'Roarke's always been more driven by personal loyalties than he lets on. Than either of us realized for a long time."

"Yes, but I suppose I tend to think of him as being more of a cynic than you."

"My darling, in many ways he's the most burning idealist of all of us."

"I think I still tend to see him as invulnerable. And not blinded by wanting to see the best in people. Though he'd be quick to say he missed the truth about his own wife."

"I can't say I saw it either."

"You're perceptive, Malcolm. But you tend to give people the benefit of the doubt until you have reason to do otherwise. I've always loved how you see the best in people."

"And you think O'Roarke is quicker to question them?"

"Sometimes. I just hope—I hope learning the truth about me—and Raoul—hasn't made it hard for you to trust." Even as she said the words, she realized how foolish they sounded. Because how could those revelations not affect his ability to trust?

"You've changed me in a number of ways, beloved. But I wouldn't say I can't trust. I trust you."

His gaze told her he was still the man he'd always been. That he'd made the choice to be so because anything else was unthinkable. Mélanie swallowed. Trust, as she'd noted before, was both a wondrous gift and a terrifying burden.

Malcolm pressed a kiss to her forehead. "In any case, whoever Weston is, I want to learn who's trying to blackmail him. And why."

"Malcolm." Mélanie scanned her husband's face. "If it is to do with the League—"

"I know. I should talk to Gelly. But I want to be more certain before I risk communicating with her."

Malcolm's sister Gisèle had been undercover with the League since January. Malcolm didn't talk about it much, but Mélanie knew he was at once baffled by her decision, worried about her safety, and fiercely proud of her. "Communicating with her has worked so far," she said.

"Because we've been careful. It's such a relief every time I see her, but I know what risks we're running. As a brother, I want to use any excuse to assure myself that she's all right. As an agent—God, I suppose a spymaster—I know to be careful when I risk meeting with an asset. I imagine Raoul once felt similarly about you."

She swallowed. "Yes. But I don't think he was as worried. Because I was with you."

"You went on missions before you married me. I don't know how he did it. And I don't mean moral compromise. I mean how the hell he lived with the fear."

"Raoul would say he's always been ruthless. And able to compartmentalize."

"Raoul would say a lot. But we both know damn well now how much of that is a façade."

Only a few months ago Raoul had admitted to pacing the floor when she was on missions. "I think he'd also say he knew I needed to make my own decisions and run my own risks. That to try to stop me would have risked destroying me and would have certainly destroyed our relationship."

"You'd been through an unimaginable hell." Malcolm's arms tightened round her and for a moment she knew he was thinking of all the things he hadn't been able to protect her from. "Gelly—"

"She hasn't seen her family killed. She hasn't been brutalized by soldiers. But, like you, she didn't have the easiest childhood.

And she's a woman trying to forge a path in a world that doesn't offer women a lot of avenues. We don't know precisely what's driving her. But I trust her enough to think she wouldn't be doing what she's doing if she didn't feel it was important."

"My sister is running appalling risks."

"Which she chose to run and would never forgive you for trying to protect her from."

Malcolm glanced across the room at one of the framed theatrical prints. Prospero and Miranda. "There's more to it than just fighting the League. Something drove her to do this now. She as good as admitted it. But she won't tell me what."

"Perhaps she will in time, when she trusts that you respect her choices. Even if you don't agree with them."

"And in the meantime, she's in constant danger."

"Which you have to trust her to be able to handle. Trust works both ways, my love."

CHAPTER 3

*a*rchibald Davenport shifted the two-week-old baby asleep in the curve of his arm and peered at the blackmail note he was holding one-handed. "I don't recognize the hand. But the capitals make it difficult. And I couldn't claim to recognize the handwriting of most of the League."

Archie had recently married Malcolm's aunt Frances. He was in the unique position of having been an Elsinore League member himself for thirty-some years, though for most of that time he'd been passing information about the League on to Raoul and to Malcolm's mother. He had also passed on information to Raoul to use in Ireland and in France and Spain.

"We don't want you to run any risks," Mélanie said. She had Philip, the other of Archie and Frances's new twins, in her arms. Frances was upstairs spending a quiet moment with nine-year-old Chloe.

Archie smoothed baby Francesca's feathery fair hair. "That's not a way any of us can allow ourselves to think. But though I can't precisely say I've been thrown out of the League, it's more or less tacitly acknowledged that as Frances's husband I can't play much of a role anymore. When I see members at Brooks's or about town, I get good-natured teasing about my downfall as a married man. I reply that they don't know my good fortune—which is quite true. They laugh, and we all pretend to still be friends. And I'm simply not invited to their gatherings anymore."

"What do you know about Weston?" Malcolm asked.

"Not a great deal. I never knew he helped the United Irishmen." Archie flicked a glance at Raoul.

"Sorry," Raoul said.

"No need to apologize. I'd be a bit disappointed if I stopped learning you had secrets. There was no need for me to know. Better for Weston that I didn't." He tucked a fold of blanket more closely about Francesca. "Weston definitely isn't the sort for the Elsinore League. Even granted there are probably members we don't know about, whose identity would surprise us, I can't imagine he's one. Definitely not the sort for carousing. He seemed loyal to his wife. Yes, I know we said that about Carfax, but at least we knew Carfax was a spymaster."

"And in retrospect we shouldn't have been surprised at how far he was willing to go in search of intelligence," Raoul said.

"And since Lady Weston's death, I haven't heard so much as a rumor about Weston and anyone else. But though I don't know much about Weston," Archie continued, "I do know something to tie Lady Darlington to the League." He coughed. Archie had quite a past, but, despite or perhaps because of it, discretion when it came to a lady's reputation was ingrained in him. "She had an affair with Alistair."

"Good God," Malcolm said. He had few illusions about his putative father, Alistair Rannoch, one of the Elsinore League's founders, but Alistair could still surprise him.

"I didn't know," Raoul said.

"Years ago. After Ireland. When you were abroad. She hadn't been long married." Archie frowned. "God knows I wasn't immune to those games, but I always felt Alistair took advantage of a young bride who hadn't necessarily made the choice to indulge in such intrigues. I don't think the affair lasted long, but I think she took it more seriously than anyone should have taken involvement with Alistair."

"Did others in the League know?" Malcolm asked.

"I'm quite sure they did. Alistair tended to talk about his conquests. I knew, and Alistair and I were hardly confidants." Archie's mouth tightened. "I remember finding her in tears in Lady Chivers's garden one night when the affair was beginning to run its course. She claimed it was over a torn flounce. I gave her a handkerchief and told her some gowns, however charming they appeared, weren't worth the fuss, and that she'd look lovely whatever she chose to wear."

He got up, started to give Francesca to Malcolm, then instead turned to Raoul. "Why don't you practice?"

Raoul raised a brow, then gave a smile that was almost sheepish. He took the baby carefully, but without noticeable worry. Francesca stirred slightly, but stayed asleep. Raoul slid a hand under her head with instinctive ease. But then, Malcolm realized, Raoul must have held Malcolm himself as a baby, if not others. Quite a bit, he now knew from stories about his childhood.

"You don't think Lady Darlington might have given the letters to the League?" Malcolm asked.

"Interesting theory." Archie turned from the bookcase. "I have no reason to think she's stayed connected to the League."

"After the revelations about Margaret last autumn, I wouldn't rule anything out." Raoul shifted his hand under Francesca's head as she stirred.

Archie frowned down at the book he had just taken from the shelf. "That's what I thought, the dates match. Would Weston have known about the Craanford business?"

Raoul's gaze locked on Archie's own while he rocked the baby slightly in his arm. "He'd have had to. He was giving us information that was vital to it."

Archie continued to hold his friend's gaze. "Don't tell n you've never thought of it."

"Of course I've thought of it." Raoul tucked the blanket round Francesca. "It's my trade to play out scenarios and after the Craanford business I played out every one I could think of. But there was nothing to tie Weston to it. Just because he changed his politics later doesn't mean he was betraying us then."

"What happened at Craanford?" Malcolm asked.

"Information went astray," Raoul said. "We lost a cache of arms and Ned Wrotham was arrested. Which probably saved his life, as it meant he missed out on the actual uprising, but at the time it was a great blow. I questioned everyone involved, including Weston. I could never determine whom the leak might have come from."

Archie returned to his chair. "Carfax was never able to determine I was behind the Dunboyne affair."

"True enough," Raoul said. "But you're an extremely skilled agent."

"If Weston pulled this off, he would be as well. Which I'll grant he doesn't seem on the surface. Which could mean one of two things."

"If he was an informant and the League knew, you'd think the League would see him as an ally rather than targeting him," Mélanie said.

"So you would," Archie said. "Though God knows alliances can fracture within the League. The League don't always follow what one would call conventional political lines. And they've certainly proven themselves capable of turning on a former ally for the most pragmatic of reasons."

"How much do you think Weston told Lady Darlington? Anne Somercote," Malcolm said.

Both Raoul and Archie looked at him. "All right," Malcolm said, aware that his wife was looking at him as well, "I confess it's a way ıclined to run. But he obviously was writing to her

ıities with the United Irishmen."

lidn't realize until last night." Raoul frowned. "If he was writing to her in enough detail to implicate him now, it's certainly possible she had the Craanford information. She's one person I didn't look into at the time. In truth, I only had the vaguest awareness of Weston's involvement with her."

"Hard to see how that could relate to someone's trying to get Weston to resign now, though," Archie said.

"No, but it might explain how whoever took the letters knew Lady Darlington had them," Mélanie said.

"Because the thief is the person she gave the information to twenty years ago?" Raoul said. "Which would narrow the suspects down to someone with government connections."

"Please don't say you're suggesting Carfax is behind the blackmail," Malcolm said.

"Doesn't really seem like his style, does it?" Raoul said.

"No," Malcolm said, picturing his former spymaster. "He's totally capable of resorting to blackmail, but he'd be far more likely to call on Weston and blackmail him to his face."

"There are plenty in the League with government and military connections," Archie said.

"If Lady Darlington was passing along information on the United Irishmen, it could add a layer to her affair with Alistair," Malcolm said.

"She wasn't quite the victim I thought she was?" Archie asked. "Possible. Like Raoul, if Weston was the traitor, I didn't see it if she was. But then, if she was very talented I might not have done."

"Possibly," Malcolm said. "But I don't lightly discount how insightful either of you is."

"Alistair was working against the United Irishmen," Raoul said. "He had Margaret reporting to him. I could see him playing on the feelings of a young woman, making her think she was doing her patriotic duty. It's possible Lady Darlington—Miss Somercote—

was giving information to Alistair before the Uprising, but they didn't become lovers until later. It's also, of course, possible we're wrong about all of this and neither Lady Darlington nor Weston had anything to do with the leak." Francesca was awake and gave a small squawk. Raoul rubbed a finger against her knuckles so she could grasp hold of it. "Whether or not Lady Darlington was passing secrets, we have to account for how the blackmailer knew to look for Weston's letters."

"The fact that he and Lady Darlington had been in love may not have been such a secret," Mélanie said. "You knew on the periphery, but you were very focused on the uprising. Perhaps Weston confided more in others or Miss Somercote did. An enemy of Weston's might have thought to go through her papers. Though it does seem a stretch, without suspecting Weston had something to hide."

"Which brings us back to Matt Trenor," Raoul said.

"Wrotham and some of the other former United Irishmen may have ideas at least as far as who may have known about the letters" Raoul lifted Francesca against his shoulder. "As usual, when one pulls a single thread a great deal of the past starts to unravel."

MALCOLM, MÉLANIE, AND RAOUL LEFT FRANCES AND ARCHIE'S house in South Audley Street on foot. The parts of their exchange with Archie lingered with the sort of reverberations Mélanie had found blessedly lacking the night before, but Raoul merely said, "Archie's given us some good leads. I should talk to Wrotham and others. And go back to Weston to see who may have known about his attachment to Lady Darlington."

Malcolm nodded. "We should get back to Berkeley Square. Harry and Cordy will be there soon."

Harry Davenport, Archie's nephew, had been a brilliant agent in the Peninsula, and his wife Cordelia was not only now an excellent investigator, she had enviable connections within the beau monde. Malcolm and Mélanie had sent word to them that morning asking them to call in Berkeley Square. They needed reinforcements.

"I'll see you in Berkeley Square later today," Raoul said.

"Raoul—" Malcolm paused on the pavement.

"I'll keep an eye out for any more ruffians. But it's Mayfair in broad daylight."

"Someone shot a gun through our window in Mayfair in broad daylight three months ago."

"A point. But I don't think we have to worry about Carfax just now."

"All the same."

"My dear Malcolm. I always guard my back."

They parted ways, Raoul heading towards Wrotham's in Upper Grosvenor Street, Mélanie and Malcolm back to Berkeley Square.

"It was a good thought about Lady Darlington," Mélanie said as she and Malcolm turned down Farm Street, her voice keyed to go neither too sharp nor too flat.

Malcolm paused to nod to Frank Storbridge, a parliamentary colleague, who was passing on the opposite side of the street. "It could mean nothing. But it's worth examining all the options."

"Yes, quite."

He paused for a moment and looked down at her. "Given recent events, I'd be a fool if I weren't particularly keenly aware that just about anyone can take information. Which is probably why I was questioning Weston's motives last night. That doesn't mean I'm questioning the people closest to me. Or if I was for a bit, it's only to have decided it was folly to do so." He put a hand over her own where it was curled round his arm. "This whole thing has made me a better agent. That's one advantage."

A laugh choked her throat. "Oh, darling."

"Surely we've learned we have to laugh, sweetheart. It's the

only way to cope with the insanity of life. In
be being perceptive to suspect Weston or Lad
as likely I'm jumping at shadows."

"You don't tend to jump at shadows, Malc
of the most perceptive people I know."

"I didn't see the truth about you."

She swallowed. She'd walked into that. "You did eventually."

"And I may now be overreacting because of it."

They turned into the Mews and then went a short distance
along Hill Street, where Harry and Cordy lived, to Berkeley
Square. A faint breeze had come up, tugging at the ribbons on her
bonnet. The breeze was crisp but the sun was warm on her face. It
gleamed off the pavement and the sparkling windows, polished
brass doorknobs, and glossily painted doors. Flowers spilled from
window boxes. The plane trees in the square garden were thick
with leaves. Springtime in London. Beautiful in a way that
brought an ache to her throat.

She turned her hand to squeeze his fingers where they still
rested on her own. "It gives us another avenue to explore. It's as
well we're exploring all of them."

"And a good thing we'll have Harry and Cordy to help us. We
could use some outside perspective."

"Not to mention help with the beau monde," Mélanie said,
making her voice light. "My one regret about our current
delightful life. We sometimes need entrée for investigations."

"Cordy and Harry are living more quietly themselves."

"Yes, but Cordy grew up at the heart of the beau monde. And
unlike you and Harry, she didn't spend her childhood and youth
hiding in the library."

～

"AN INVESTIGATION," CORDELIA DAVENPORT SAID ACROSS THE

Square breakfast table. "And to think I thought we'd
the week absorbed by wedding plans."

"Hardly elaborate wedding plans," Laura said.

"Just because it's small doesn't mean it can't be memorable. In
fact, it will be all the more memorable without a lot of stuffy
protocol."

Miles Addison, Malcolm's valet, frowned into his coffee cup.
He was hearing the story for the first time, along with his wife
Blanca, who had their five-month-old son in her lap. Both were
accomplished investigators in their own right. "Do you want me
to have a word with the Darlingtons' servants? Discreetly?
Someone may have noticed something the night of the ball."

"That would be most helpful," Malcolm said.

"I can go with you," Blanca said. She glanced at Laura.

"Of course I can watch Pedro," Laura said.

Mélanie picked up the coffeepot to refill the cups. "Do you
know Lady Darlington, Cordy?"

Cordelia took a sip of coffee. "Not well, but she and my
mother are acquainted. Though since she's agreed to help, for
once we won't need connections to get us in the door."

"The guests from her ball may be more challenging," Mélanie
said. "I'm likely to need your help."

Cordelia reached for the milk jug. "Dearest, you couldn't keep
me away from this. It's very agreeable to be back in London, but I
do feel rather as though we've spent the past three months on
tenterhooks without being able to do anything."

"We're spoiled," Harry said, one eye on the hearthrug, where
Colin, Emily, and Jessica were playing with the Davenport girls,
Livia and Drusilla.

"You've wanted something to do just as much as I have,"
Cordelia said.

"I don't deny it. "

Cordelia took a sip of coffee. "Lizzy and Tom Wexford were at

the Darlington ball. Lizzy mentioned it when we saw th
theatre the next night."

"I'll talk to Tom," Harry said. "It will mean sharing regimenta
stories, but if I drop hints about a secret mission, he'll be eager to
share any information he has."

"I'm going to see Sandy Trenor," Malcolm said. "His mother is
Lady Darlington's cousin."

"Good heavens, she is," Cordelia said. "That could help. Or
complicate things."

"I should call on Lady Darlington," Mélanie said. "Come with
me, Cordy?"

Cordelia swallowed the last of her coffee. "I was so hoping
you'd ask."

CHAPTER 4

*T*he Hon. Alexander Trenor's valet admitted Malcolm to a smart set of rooms in Piccadilly and showed him into the sitting room. Sandy was not at home, but Bet Simcox came forwards with a shy smile as Malcolm entered the room.

"Thank you, Birchley," she said after the briefest hesitation. She was not used to having servants. "Perhaps you could bring us some tea."

"Of course, miss." Birchley's tone was warm and respectful, Malcolm was relieved to see, and also held a note of kindness. He smiled at Bet as he left the room. Bet smiled back.

"You look well," Malcolm said. Bet wore a simple muslin dress with a peach-colored sash and her fair hair was pulled back at the nape of her neck. She might have been any young wife, still a bit uncertain about being mistress of her own home and receiving her husband's friends. But she wasn't Sandy's wife, she was his mistress. Less than four months ago, she had lived in rooms in St. Giles where, until Sandy, she had entertained numerous clients to keep bread on her table. Yet she and Sandy were in love with all the impetuous ardor of youth, in the my-bounty-is-as-boundlessas-the-sea way that Malcolm had been too old for long before he met Mélanie.

"I usually make myself scarce when Sandy's friends call," Bet said. "But you're different."

"Not the least because I'm your friend as well."

Bet smiled. "It's very odd, my living here. I kept saying I'd leave as soon as it was safe, but Sandy didn't want me to, and after Matt was arrested, it seemed to help him that I was here."

"I'm sure it did," Malcolm said.

"I hope so." Bet moved to a chintz-covered straight-backed chair, as though she had suddenly realized Malcolm couldn't sit until she did so. "It's been hard, you know that. I thought it got a bit easier when Matt was gone." She looked down at her hands. "Sandy wouldn't say goodbye to Matt."

"Matthew Trenor held you at knifepoint," Malcolm said. The memory of that scene, in this very room, was still sharp within him.

"But that was because he was trying to escape. It wasn't to do with me. I tried to tell Sandy that. He said that was the problem. That Matt wasn't thinking of me as a person at all. Or thinking of the girl he killed as a person either."

"He was right."

"About me. Matt just wanted to escape that night. He was desperate and willing to do anything and he thought grabbing me would get him out of the room. Out of the country. But I think he did think of Miranda Dormer as a person. A person he cared about. Men do, you know, even with girls they—" She broke off, flushing.

"I do know," Malcolm said, his gaze steady. "Though not from personal experience. Matthew didn't care about Miranda Dormer the way Sandy cares about you, but I think you're right he did care about her. But he killed her anyway."

"He thought she was going to betray him."

Funny, the echoes a word could carry. "Yes, I suppose she was.

In that she was going to reveal that he'd been committing treason. Which is a betrayal in and of itself."

"But they're still brothers. That's what I tried to tell Sandy. It will matter to him someday that he didn't say goodbye to Matt."

Malcolm thought of his own brother and the tangle of things they had never really said to each other and most likely never would. "You're more important to Sandy than his brother. I can't argue with that. In the circumstances, I commend it."

Bet shook her head. "Matt will always be his brother. I don't have any delusions about always when it comes to Sandy and me."

"Don't you?" Malcolm smiled at her. "I think perhaps you underrate both of you."

Bet flushed and shook her head. "You're kind, Mr. Rannoch."

"My dear girl. I didn't say it to be kind."

She shook her head. "His parents seem to have accepted that Matt's gone, from what he says, as much as they ever could. At least, that's what Sandy said. But Sandy seems—" She frowned. "More preoccupied, somehow. He came home from dinner with his parents a fortnight ago with the oddest look on his face. I asked him if something was wrong, though I try not to pry. I just wanted to do anything to help. And for a moment it seemed he was about to tell me something. Then it was almost as though he bit the words back, and he started talking nonsense in that way he does when he doesn't want one to realize he has as keen an under-standing as he does. He's been the same way ever since, but every so often I catch him staring into space, with the oddest look, as though he's puzzling over something. And he hasn't seemed to want to go back to see his parents except when he absolutely has to. He says they don't need him about so much now, but I can't help but wonder if there's more to it." She pleated a fold of her gown between her fingers. "Has he said anything to you?"

"No. If he confided in anyone, it's much more likely to be you. He's had a great deal to adjust to. I daresay he'll tell you when he's ready." Though Malcolm couldn't but wonder if Sandy's parents, responding to the loss of Matt, and Sandy's being in some ways their only remaining son, were pressuring him to marry. That could well be something Sandy would keep from Bet and also something that would have him avoiding his parents.

Birchley came in with the tea tray. Malcolm watched Bet pour tea into the delicate blue-flowered cups, keenly remembering her pouring brandy-laced tea into chipped mugs and glasses in her rooms in St. Giles. She held the pot with care, asked if he wanted milk or lemon, handed him the cup without sloshing the tea. He'd heard Mel one day, about two months since, giving Bet lessons in the small salon in Berkeley Square. They'd been put to good use.

Bet stirred milk into her own tea. "If you're here, something must have happened."

"Not necessarily."

"You're here without Mél—Mrs. Rannoch—and the children."

"A fair point. They'll come to see you soon. Jessica's been asking about you. We'd like to have you and Sandy to dine."

"That's very thoughtful. I know it's not appropriate—"

"Stuff, as my wife would say." Malcolm took a sip of tea. "But as it happens, I did want to talk to Sandy about one of our investigations. Lady Darlington is his mother's cousin, isn't she?"

Bet frowned. "Yes, Lady Marchmain and Lady Darlington are both granddaughters of the Marquis of Scorseby." She laughed. "That sounds odd, doesn't it? I don't go with Sandy on family outings, and I don't sit at home reading Debrett's, but I've always been a good listener. And I am curious about the people close to Sandy. I have to piece them together in my mind, since I can't meet them."

Malcolm took another sip of tea and felt as though he'd swallowed glass. One could argue the challenges he'd faced in his own relationship were nothing beside those Bet accepted so matter-of-factly. "Does Sandy talk about Lady Darlington?"

"He was complaining only last week that he had to go to

Almack's to make her happy. But he also says she's one of his kindest relations. I think—"

She broke off as the door opened, and Sandy came into the room with the brisk impetuosity of youth. "Rannoch. Birchley said you were here. Good to see you." Sandy bent to kiss Bet, then dropped down on the arm of her chair with his usual ease. But there was something contained beneath the casual movement. Almost as though he were an actor putting on a careful performance of easy nonchalance. A very good actor. Malcolm wasn't sure he'd have noticed it if it hadn't been for Bet's confidences before Sandy came into the room. "Is something afoot?" Sandy asked. "You don't usually come without Mélanie."

"Bet said the same thing. In truth, we are in the midst of a new investigation. And it may concern Lady Darlington."

"Aunt Anne? If you can get her to stop throwing eligible girls in my way, I'll be eternally grateful." Sandy frowned. "She's not in trouble, is she?"

"Some letters a young man sent her many years ago have gone missing. It was before her marriage, but they could do harm to the gentleman in question."

"Good God." Sandy stared at Malcolm. "Sorry. It's just—one doesn't think of one's parents and their generation—"

Anne Darlington was probably less than a decade Malcolm's senior. Malcolm hid a smile.

"People can care for people before they marry, Sandy," Bet said in a quiet voice. "It doesn't make less of the marriage."

"Mmm. Well, I can't say I'm surprised on that score. Aunt Anne and Uncle Billy never struck me as a romantic couple when Uncle Billy was alive. Not that my parents do," he added in the same carefully nonchalant tone. "Not that anyone of their generation does."

"Don't let Aunt Frances and Archie hear you say that. Or O'Roarke."

"Oh, you know what I mean. It's different with family. One's parents always seem a million years old. Can't imagine thinking of Lady Frances as old. Or Archie or O'Roarke. But Aunt Anne's always been such a high stickler. Friends with the patronesses of Almack's. Shouldn't be surprised if she joined them if there's an opening."

Which, considering the behavior of Emily Cowper and Dorothea Lieven, both patronesses, wasn't ruling out a lot Lady Darlington might have done or might be doing.

Bet poured another cup of tea and put it in Sandy's hand. Sandy stared into it for a moment, then took a sip. "Aunt Anne looks askance if I wear trousers instead of knee breeches. Can't imagine her—Always been kind to me, though. Damn sight sweeter than my mother. And she was quick to call on Mama after Matt—after Matt was arrested. Didn't worry about the scandal like some, for all she's high in the instep." He stared at Malcolm. "Is this something to do with this Elsinore League?"

"It may be."

"Was this man Aunt Anne loved one of them?"

"No, they appear to be targeting him."

Sandy scraped a hand over his hair. "Once—I overheard her tell Mama that her—that is Aunt Anne's—life could have been so very different. One doesn't think about parents and uncles and aunts regretting where they are. One doesn't think about them making choices at all. They simply are who they are."

"Born fully formed like Botticelli's Venus?"

"Yes. No—that is—not at all like Venus." Sandy scraped a hand through his hair. "But one doesn't think about them having a past. Any sort of past, that is."

"Yes, I remember Colin being quite confused about Mel's referring to something that happened before he was born." And now, of course, Colin was navigating the complicated story of his own parentage.

Sandy reached for his teacup. "Who's the man in question?"

It was Malcolm's turn to hesitate.

"I can't help you if I don't know," Sandy pointed out. "I might know something about him. For God's sake, Rannoch, I'm not going to go about spreading tales about my aunt."

"No, of course you wouldn't." Malcolm turned his cup in his hand. "Do you know Lord Weston?"

"Of course I—" Sandy stared at him. "Good God. He and Aunt Anne—"

"They once hoped to marry. Lack of fortune was a problem for both."

"So she married Uncle Billy. That explains a lot."

Bet frowned. "But surely they weren't completely without resources—Nan and Sam don't have anything and they're remarkably happy."

"It's not the same," Sandy said. "They couldn't live on next to nothing like your sister and Sam do. They'd need money for a house, for servants, you know the sort of thing."

"So she had to marry a man she didn't care for?"

"At least not the man she loved," Malcolm said.

"But now Lord Weston has money?" Bet said.

"Yes, it's rather ironic," Malcolm said.

"I wonder if she wishes she'd waited for him," Sandy said. He splashed milk into his tea. "Trying to remember if I ever saw her with Weston. Must have done. They both go to my parents' parties. Poor Aunt Anne."

"Did you ever hear Lady Darlington mention Alistair Rannoch?"

Sandy frowned. "She wasn't—"

Malcolm drew a breath. A lady's reputation, a young man's sensibilities, versus the truth. "She may have been close to him at one point. And, as you know, he was one of the founders of the League."

"But he's been dead for almost two years."

"Yes, it may have nothing to do with this business now. But any connection to the League is interesting."

Sandy ran a hand over his hair. "Alistair Rannoch used to dine with my parents. Usually without your mother. I didn't pay much heed because it was mostly when I was in the schoolroom or at Eton or Oxford. But I remember Mama once asking me to go to the dining room to change round the cards, because she said she'd made a mistake. She'd had Aunt Anne sitting beside Alistair Rannoch and instead she had me move Aunt Anne to the other end of the table. I was curious enough I watched them at dinner. Aunt Anne didn't seem to want to meet Mr. Rannoch's gaze." Sandy continued to frown. "Aunt Anne was close to him how?"

Malcolm kept his gaze steady of Sandy's face. "We don't know precisely."

"Oh, Christ." Sandy's pale complexion went white as his cravat. "I mean, I know people—"

"It's only hearsay," Malcolm said. Which was true, leaving aside that Archie was a very reliable source.

Sandy shook his head. "It's not that I had any particular illusions about her marriage to Uncle Billy. And from what you tell me she wasn't that keen to marry him in the first place. But—so the reason someone wants Weston's letters to Aunt Anne has something to do with her having a—a liaison with Alistair Rannoch?"

"Possibly. It's possible that she told Alistair about Weston's letters and that's how the League knew to look for them. It's possible it's a coincidence."

"You don't like coincidences."

"No, I don't." Malcolm set down his teacup and got to his feet. "I need hardly impress on you the need to keep quiet about this."

"Of course. I'd understand that even if it weren't to do with my family." Sandy stood as well. "You'll tell us if we can help?"

"That goes without saying," Malcolm said. He clasped Sandy's hand and kissed Bet's cheek. "If not before, we'll see you at the wedding."

"Of course," Sandy said.

"I'll—" Bet hesitated. "Sandy will represent us."

"Bet!" Sandy said.

"Laura and Raoul will miss you if you aren't there," Malcolm said. "They're the last people to give any heed to what the world think of anyone. Not that any of us does."

"It's different," Bet said. "They're both part of society."

Laura and Raoul would both claim they were on the edges of society—as in many ways Malcolm and Mélanie were now—but, meeting Bet's gaze, Malcolm recognized there was a world of difference. An unconscionable world, but not one he could wish away like a conjurer from one of his children's story books. "The wedding is hardly a society occasion," Malcolm said. "But it is an occasion for friends. Besides"—he smiled—"the children will never forgive you—or us—if you aren't there."

An answering smile crossed Bet's face. "I'd hate to disappoint the children."

"Well, then," Malcolm said, returning the smile. "We'll see you both there."

"MRS. RANNOCH. LADY CORDELIA." LADY DARLINGTON GOT TO HER feet, hand extended as though it were a purely social occasion, though her face was set with lines of strain. She wore a high-collared dress of pale blue lustring and her fair hair was pinned in an elaborate arrangement that showed the elegant bones of her face to advantage.

"I hope you don't mind that I've brought Cordelia," Mélanie said. "She and her husband often assist us."

"Not in the least." Lady Darlington busied herself pouring tea. Some people, Mélanie had noted, became even more careful of social rituals in the course of an investigation, as though it was a way to hold on to normalcy in the face of chaos. "Lady

Castlereagh speaks very fondly of you, Mrs. Rannoch," she said, handing Mélanie an eggshell cup and saucer rimmed in gold.

Mélanie smoothed the bottle green sarcenet of her gown. She had chosen it carefully for its demure ruffles and high collar. The sort of gown she would have worn to pay calls as a political wife. "She's been very kind to me."

"She said she quite depended on you in Vienna, when a simple seating arrangement had international implications." Lady Darlington squeezed a wedge of lemon into her own tea. "We haven't seen you about as much since your return to Britain."

"No, I've been spending time with my children and writing a great deal."

Lady Darlington gave a polite smile that managed to still register amazement that Mélanie could fill her time with writing and her children. "Ah, yes. I forgot you help your husband with his speeches."

"And I write articles. And I've been working on a few other projects." Mélanie smiled and took a sip of tea. No need to wrap her life up in a veneer of what passed for normalcy in the beau monde, as she once would have done. A bit silly when Laura and Raoul's situation left them—thank goodness—on the edges of the polite world, and when Malcolm had assured her that he didn't need a hostess at the heart of things for the sake of his career. Lady Castlereagh was a patroness of Almack's. Though Mélanie had seen her since their return to Britain and Lady Castlereagh had been perfectly civil, she had not invited the Rannochs to her home or mentioned Almack's. Emily Cowper, another patroness, had assured Mélanie she could procure vouchers for her should Mélanie wish to attend the assemblies. Since Mélanie had no particular wish to do so (particularly as Malcolm would almost certainly resist accompanying her), she saw no need to ask Emily to make use of her social capital.

Lady Darlington stirred her tea. "I'm sure that keeps you busy.

But it's a pity. You have formidable talents as a hostess, my dear. I hate to see them go to waste."

"She has formidable talents at a great many things," Cordelia said.

"Such as investigations." Lady Darlington took a sip of tea. For a moment, Mélanie suspected she wished her cup contained something stronger. "My cousin Helen says you've been very kind to her."

"Lady Marchmain has been through a great deal," Mélanie said. "And I realize that an investigation of Malcolm's and mine set those events in motion."

"One can hardly blame you for exposing Matthew's crimes," Lady Darlington said, with a bluntness that surprised Mélanie. "For all Helen's grief, I don't believe even she would do so. It's been a terrible shock. Alexander at least has been behaving quite sensibly. I believe you are acquainted with him."

Mélanie smiled at Lady Darlington over the rim of her teacup. "We're very fond of him."

"He's taken up with an unfortunate young woman, but I don't expect that will last very long."

Mélanie swallowed a pang at the thought of what the future most likely held for Sandy and Bet. "We're very fond of her as well," she said. A year ago she might have hesitated to address the issue so bluntly with a woman in Lady Darlington's position. Which rather shamed her now.

Lady Darlington raised her brows. "Surely—"

"More important, Sandy's very fond of her. And quite happy, I think."

"My dear Mrs. Rannoch. You have children—"

"Colin and Jessica are also very attached to Bet."

"She's—"

"The woman Sandy loves."

Lady Darlington shook her head. "Gentlemen have their

adventures before they marry. Afterwards as well, in some cases. But to have set her up in his own rooms—"

"It seems rather sensible." Cordelia reached for a lemon biscuit. "Why spend money on a second establishment. You could say Sandy is being frugal."

Lady Darlington choked on her tea. "Of all the things I've heard Sandy called in the family, frugal is not on the list." She turned her cup on its saucer. "He's had a lot of burdens placed on his shoulders all at once. To all intents and purposes he's the heir now. Not to the title, but I know Marchmain has arranged to leave most of the property to Alexander. I suppose—if this girl makes Sandy happy for the present, I should be grateful for that. I'm hardly in a position to cast aspersions." She set down her cup and folded her hands in her lap. "As Lord Weston has told you, the letters—private letters he wrote to me when we were both young —must have disappeared at my ball a fortnight ago."

"It's a dreadful invasion of your privacy, ma'am," Cordelia said.

"I never thought—It never occurred to me such things could be deemed important so many years later to anyone but Lord Weston and myself. Foolish, perhaps, to have kept the letters, but they— meant a great deal to me." She reached her cup. Her fingers curled round the handle. "Algy—Lord Weston, that is—and I hoped to marry. We considered ourselves betrothed when he wrote those letters. But I had very little in the way of a dowry. And Algy—Lord Weston—had few prospects at that time. My father said I'd be dooming myself to a life of privation if I married him. I said I wouldn't mind, of course. But to complicate matters, Algy had an uncle who was willing to sponsor him at one of the Inns of the Court but who wanted him to make the right marriage to a girl with a dowry. My mother told me I was doing Algy a disservice by hurting his prospects. I held out for quite a while. At that age, one can be so convinced that one can forge the future one wants, whatever the obstacles. But I have three younger sisters. When Lord Darlington offered for me, I could not but be aware of how advantageous it would be for our whole family. Algy said I must not reproach myself. That he could offer me nothing. Of course, as things turned out—" She shook her head, dislodging a carefully pinned curl. "But it is folly to refine upon what cannot be changed. I have my dear children. Lord Weston has his lovely daughters. That's why it's so particularly dreadful to think I could be the cause of upsetting his happiness. Of damaging his daughters' prospects. Of confounding the work that means so much to him." She took a quick sip of tea. "It's been years since we fancied ourselves in love, but one doesn't stop caring."

"Of course not," Mélanie said. "I quite understand." Though she did wonder if, both widowed, Lady Darlington and Weston had any thoughts of a future together.

"Do you? At your age, I think I was convinced a new love would quite drive an old from memory. Life is so very much more complicated than it seems when one is twenty or even five-and-twenty." Lady Darlington took a quick sip of tea. Her smile was tranquil. Her gaze held regret. "When I first realized the letters were missing, I confess my worry was for how it might distress my children if they became public. Or Lord Weston's children. That's what I went to Lord Weston about. It was only when I saw his reaction that I realized the—wider implications." She set down her cup. Her hands locked together in her lap. "Who could want to do this to him? He's such a good man."

"Men in power have enemies," Mélanie said. "Someone might think they could gain from Lord Weston's being removed from power without having any personal anger at Lord Weston at all."

"It's monstrous."

"Yes. Blackmail for whatever reason is always unpleasant." Not that she'd been above employing such tactics herself in extreme circumstances. "Lady Darlington," she added, in the tones she'd use when broaching an uncomfortable topic with her children, "I believe you have a list of the guests at the ball."

"Oh, yes. Of course." Lady Darlington got to her feet and

moved to a gilded, spindle-legged escritoire. She lifted a sealed paper from the blotter, but then stood holding it, fingers taut on the cream laid.

"I know it seems dreadfully like sharing secrets," Cordelia said. "But when a crime's been committed the rules do change, ma'am."

"Yes. Of course. I just don't want to make things awkward for any of my guests."

"One of your guests is making things exceedingly awkward for you and Lord Weston, Lady Darlington," Mélanie said. "But I assure you that my husband and I and the Davenports and Mr. O'Roarke have no wish to disturb anyone's peace. We'll be as discreet as possible. We're quite good at it."

Lady Darlington gave a slow nod and put the paper into Mélanie's hand. "I couldn't bear it if anything happened to Algy."

"Lady Darlington." Mélanie took a sip of tea. Delicately scented, but a bit less strong than she preferred it. "Forgive my being blunt. As I said, we'll be as discreet as we can. But to recover the papers, we need all the information possible."

Lady Darlington drew back a fraction against the fringed chintz cushions in her chair. "You have a list of the guests."

"I'm not thinking of the present in this case. I'm thinking of the past." Mélanie set down her teacup. "Archibald Davenport mentioned that at one time you might have been rather closely acquainted with Alistair Rannoch."

Lady Darlington's cup tilted in her fingers. She righted it just before tea spattered all over her skirt. "Of course I was acquainted with your husband's father. And with Lady Arabella. Not well, but we saw them at parties, and we dined with them on occasion."

"Archie believes it may have been a bit more with Mr. Rannoch." Cordelia leaned forwards. "Forgive me, Lady Darlington. You know I am no stranger to scandal. Archie was most concerned for your reputation. As are we."

Lady Darlington returned her teacup to the satinwood table with a clink. "I don't see how this ancient history—which is all a farrago of nonsense, in any case—has anything to do with the missing letters from Algy."

Mélanie drew a breath. One might say there was too much secrecy about the Elsinore League. But it was also dangerous information to share. "We have reason to believe that the enemies of Lord Weston's who took the letters may be part of a club of which Alistair Rannoch was a member."

"And you think—"

"We don't know what to think yet. Save that any connection to Lord Weston could be important."

Lady Darlington put a hand to her head and jabbed a pin into her perfectly coiffed curls. "I told you my father wouldn't hear of my marrying Algy. That at last I realized the benefits to my family if I accepted Lord Darlington's very obliging offer. I was not coerced, you understand. Not in any way. I was very sensible of what I owed Lord Darlington. But I can't claim my affections were engaged to the point of—"

"It was not a love match," Cordelia said.

"No." Lady Darlington folded her hands in her lap. "And Lord Darlington had no illusions that it was, any more than I did. Indeed, I believe I think he would have considered anything else vulgar."

But Lady Darlington, by her own admission, had been in love and wanted to marry the man she loved, only months before her marriage to Lord Darlington. "It can be difficult to begin a marriage," Mélanie said. "I know it was so for me." Particularly as she had been spying on her husband and lying about her entire background.

"And leaving Ireland I imagine you were lonely," Cordelia said. "London society isn't always the friendliest place. Especially for a young bride."

"No." Lady Darlington's fingers locked tighter, her knuckles white. "Lord Darlington went to a shooting party in Norfolk shortly after we were married. The sort of party that is for gentlemen only. I stayed in London for the Little Season. I had plenty of invitations but few close friends. One does find parties difficult to navigate at first. I was rather inclined to sit on a settee. These days I'm always on the lookout for young wives who do that and try to introduce them about. At the time, I confess I was very grateful for Mr. Rannoch's kind attentions."

"I can quite see how it must have been," Mélanie said.

Lady Darlington's gaze locked on Mélanie's own across the tea table. "Can you, Mrs. Rannoch?" She reached for her cup and took a determined sip. "I'm a loyal wife. I wasn't the sort to—seek diversion."

"Unlike me," Cordelia said in crisp tones. "No sense wrapping it up in clean linen. Happy as Harry and I are now, there's no denying I made a mockery of my marriage vows at one time. But the thing is, ma'am, wild as I may have been considered, even I didn't start out intending to do so. It happens by degrees. One is lonely. One seeks escape. One finds oneself taking a turn about the garden with a gentleman because it's a way to escape the tedium of the ballroom and pleasant to have someone to talk to. One lingers outside because the candlelit crowds inside can be horribly lonely. One thing leads to another."

"Alistair Rannoch was a difficult man," Mélanie said. "But he could be very charming."

"He was kind. Or I thought he was." Lady Darlington straightened her shoulders and reached for her teacup. "We weren't—friendly—for very long. Even then I knew it was madness. It was only after we'd—called an end to things—that I learned it had all been because of a wager."

Mélanie clunked her cup down in its saucer. "Gentlemen, at least some of them, who really aren't gentlemen at all, have a great deal to answer for. Do you know whom the wager was with?"

Lady Darlington hesitated. "Lord Beverston."

One of the founders and current leaders of the League. Whose name Mélanie had just noted on the list of guests at the ball where the letters disappeared. "Did you say anything to Mr. Rannoch about Lord Weston?" Mélanie asked.

"I'd hardly have spoken with him about another man."

"One does sometimes," Cordelia said. "Spilling one's heart out can be a way of bonding, oddly."

Lady Darlington's brows drew together. "I don't remember speaking about Algy to Alistair—Mr. Rannoch. I did confess I was —that I had found less happiness in my marriage than I had hoped, though I thought I had gone into it with few illusions." She gave an unexpected, twisted smile. "I thought myself quite a sophisticated woman of the world. In truth, looking back, I was little more than a child." She frowned again. "I can't swear to it, but I don't think Alistair had the least idea Algy had been anything to me until later."

"Later?" Mélanie froze in the midst of reaching for her cup.

"Yes. I assume he knew that at the time of the duel."

Mélanie rarely betrayed surprise, but this time she could not contain it. "Lord Weston and Alistair fought a duel?"

"Yes, surely—" Lady Darlington bit back her words.

"Lord Weston didn't tell us," Mélanie said. "But believe me, Lady Darlington, this is precisely the sort of thing we need to know. It could prove to be vital to getting the letters back."

"But obviously Alistair didn't take the letters—"

"No, but his friends may have done."

Lady Darlington drew a sharp breath. "Alistair and I called an end to things, as I said. I was telling myself I'd had a fortunate escape when I overheard—from some women I counted friends —that I had been the subject of a wager between Alistair and Lord Beverston."

"Men can be appalling," Cordelia said. "But so can women. Some men and some women. There are reasons I'm glad to escape the beau monde."

"It can be an uncomfortable place," said the woman who was one of its arbiters. "Especially when one isn't at the heart of things. Which I wasn't. Not then." She snatched up her teacup and took a swallow. "I should have left well enough alone. But less than a fortnight later, Lord Weston came to town. We were faultlessly polite, but he could tell something was wrong. I denied it at first, but when he started to suspect Lord Darlington had been unkind I had to defend my husband (about whom I was already feeling guilty enough) and then the whole wretched story tumbled out. I kept insisting he should simply let it go, but he was furious, and I confess a part of me was gratified to have a champion. Not that it ever occurred to me—" She took another quick swallow. "He never told me what he intended. It was my maid, who knew Lord Weston's valet, who told me about the duel. I begged Algy not to meet Alistair. I told him it couldn't mend matters and the scandal would be dreadful for everyone—"

"Including you," Cordelia said.

"I didn't precisely say that, but he must have seen it. Normally Algy is the sort to be very sensitive to a woman's reputation. But he said he wouldn't ever breathe a word about the cause of the duel, but Alistair Rannoch must be held to account for his crimes. I'm sorry, Mrs. Rannoch."

"On the contrary. I imagine a number of people would agree with Lord Weston's view of Mr. Rannoch. I certainly would. But I do question the method. Did the duel actually occur?"

"Yes. Algy was wounded in the arm and confined to his bed for a fortnight—during which you can imagine how I tormented myself—though he made a complete recovery. Alistair Rannoch was unhurt." Her mouth tightened. "I understand they celebrated at breakfast afterwards."

"They?" Mélanie asked. "Do you know who his second was?"

"Lord Beverston. Despite his losing the wager to Mr. Rannoch."

"Or perhaps because of it," Cordelia said. "Gentlemen have a dreadful way of wagering about these matters with their closest friends and then being sporting in their congratulations, with no concern for the women involved."

"And Lord Weston's second?" Mélanie asked.

Lady Darlington pressed her hands in her lap. "He wouldn't tell me. But I had my maid make inquiries, so I could plead with him to stop the duel. Of course he told me it was an affair of honor between men, and I should stay out of it. Which was a bit ridiculous, considering I was the cause of it in the first place. I didn't know him well, but I do think he did his best to stop it, as much as seconds ever do. It was Sir Hugh Cresswell."

Mélanie cast a glance at Cordelia. She wasn't sure what was more surprising. The duel in and of itself, or the fact that Weston's second had also been a member of the Elsinore League.

CHAPTER 5

"Hugh Cresswell is on the guest list Lady Darlington gave us," Cordelia said. "Do you think the affair and the duel twenty years ago was all some sort of setup? Were they all in on it to entrap Lord Weston—Alistair Rannoch, Lord Beverston, and Hugh Cresswell?"

"An interesting thought." Archie frowned into his glass of port. His coat was light blue, the lines obviously tailored by Stultz, his cravat tied in a negligent style that was the unattained goal of almost every young gallant in the beau monde. The picture of a middle-aged dandy, Malcolm thought, save that once again he had a baby—Philip, this time—cuddled in his free arm. "Save that they don't seem to have got anything out of it, that we know of. In fact, potentially the reverse if they're trying to go after Weston now." His frown deepened. "I don't remember hearing about the duel at the time. Or about the wager that apparently began the affair. Not that that's entirely surprising."

"It wasn't entered in the betting book at Brooks's? Or White's?" Mélanie asked.

Archie met her gaze across his and Fanny's library in South Audley Street. "I have often lamented my friends'—or at least my associates'—lack of discretion in such matters. Partly out of concern for the reputations of the ladies involved, partly, I confess, because of the sheer vulgarity. But having daughters, not to mention granddaughters—or, I should say, great-nieces—does make one rather keenly aware of the horrors." He glanced at Francesca, now lying in Harry's lap, then towards the parlor where Chloe was playing with the older children, including Harry and Cordelia's daughters.

"You should call them granddaughters," Harry said. "And yes, it does."

Archie gave a faint smile. "Such things do get talked about. Particularly among the Elsinore League. With whom I was closely involved at the time. And I don't remember hearing anything about this."

"Nor do I," Frances said. "Ladies talk as well, you know. It's not as likely to be the subject of a wager—though you'd be surprised— but the gossip can be quite as intense and quite as deaf to the potential harm done. Indeed, at times it seems designed precisely to do harm. And I confess I know a number of women whose pastime was tearing the character of women like Lady Darlington—at least Lady Darlington as she was then—to shreds. A young wife who had all the advantages of youth and beauty—enough to stir jealousy— without having the least idea how to go on in the world or having friends to defend her. Really, Sheridan was absurdly close to the mark in *School for Scandal*, as is Simon in just about everything he writes." She frowned. "I remember Lady Darlington then. I thought her an insipid thing, I confess. I fear I wouldn't have been as sympathetic as I should, had anyone told me the story. But no one did."

"Not even Alistair?" Malcolm asked.

Frances met his gaze. Malcolm and his putative father had never been close, but Frances had had a long-term affair with Alistair Rannoch. "No. Damn the man, he has a lot to answer for."

Archie continued to frown, seemingly undisturbed by the fact that his wife was talking about her former lover, who was also his former supposed friend on whom he had spent decades spying. "It's possible Cresswell simply was Weston's friend and it's a complete coincidence he was the second in the duel." He glanced round the room. "I'm as wary of coincidences as the rest of you, but they do happen, you know. Or, as you say, it's possible he and Alistair and Beverston were playing some sort of game with Weston. But if so, it's difficult to see their objective. Weston went on to have an exemplary career."

"Until now," Raoul said.

Archie took another drink of port, carefully holding Philip steady. "The League generally aren't the sort to hold off two decades before trying again if a plan fails."

"Unless they got something from the duel we're failing to see," Malcolm said.

"What if Alistair was meant to kill Lord Weston?" Cordelia said.

"Interesting." Raoul took a sip of coffee. "Alistair was a good shot. I'd be surprised he missed if he intended to kill. But in any case, we still have the question of why the League wanted Weston out of the way and why they then waited twenty years before moving against him again."

"They've been slow when it comes to you," Laura said.

"It's been eight months, not twenty years. And I'm still not convinced they really want to get rid of me rather than using an attack on me to try to draw out Julien St. Juste."

"But that brings up another point," Harry said. "If they tried to kill Weston with the duel, they could have tried to have him killed again, without resorting to blackmail."

"Killing's a messy business," Raoul said. "I could see the League caviling at it on those grounds, if not moral ones."

"Besides," Cordelia said, "Weston only challenged Alistair Rannoch because Lady Darlington confided in him. I don't see how they could have been sure that she would. Most women would be inclined not to tell a former lover about a love affair."

"Alistair was deathly opposed to the Irish Uprising," Malcolm said. "What if he knew Weston had been involved and got close to Lady Darlington in the hope of learning something to bring Weston down?"

Raoul turned his cup in his hand. "An interesting thought. We'd have the question of how he learned Weston was involved with us. I don't put it past Alistair to have ferreted out the truth. But if so, he didn't learn about the letters from Lady Darlington then."

He looked round as the library door opened, and Frances and Archie's footman showed Addison into the room. "I'm sorry for the interruption," Addison said, "but I didn't think this should wait."

"You're hardly interrupting when you're part of the investigation," Malcolm said. "What have you learned?"

"Little to report from the Darlington staff," Addison said. "Save that Lady Darlington is well-liked by her staff, and I'd lay odds none of them sold her letters. But when Blanca and I got back to Berkeley Square, we found this." He held a sealed paper out to Malcolm. "I recognized enough to know you'd probably want to see it at once."

The handwriting, even in plain capitals, was plainly Gisèle's. Malcolm slit the seal, a plain wafer, with his nail. It was in a code he had taught her. Mélanie, glancing over his shoulder, put paper and an inkwell in his hand. He decoded the brief message in but a few minutes, his hand shaking more than he would like to admit. Gisèle had information she wanted to share with him. And she could meet him tonight.

～

WESTON GLANCED AROUND THE SALON HUNG WITH PURPLE-STRIPED

silk. "Kind of Lady Frances and Davenport to give us a place to meet."

"It seemed less obvious than my calling on you," Raoul said. "And while I could manage to get myself admitted to White's—I've done so before—that would also risk undue attention."

"You've learned something?" Weston asked.

"A number of things, though we can't fit the pieces together yet." Raoul regarded his friend. "You didn't tell us about Lady Darlington and Alistair Rannoch and the duel."

Weston's brows snapped together. "What's that to say to anything?"

"Perhaps nothing. Perhaps everything. Alistair started a group called the Elsinore League. They seek to influence events to the personal advantage of their members using a variety of tactics. Including blackmail."

"And you think they're the ones who took the letters?"

"It begins to very much look that way. What did Lady Darlington say to you about Alistair Rannoch?"

"For God's sake, O'Roarke—"

"Blackmail leaves little room for niceties. Lady Darlington understood that when she confided the story to Mrs. Rannoch. You must know your secrets are safe with me."

Weston met Raoul's gaze across Fanny's Axminster carpet. His gaze was far more wary now than that of the fresh-faced young man he'd been at five-and-twenty. "We aren't allies anymore, O'Roarke."

"You can't think I'd use personal information against a friend." Though he had spied on his own son.

"In the world you live in? I saw just how far you were willing to go for what you believed in. I admired you for it. Tell me you wouldn't have done anything if you'd have thought it would have made a difference in Ireland twenty years ago."

"Anything? No. I've always had limits, though they may be hard even for me to see. But I would have gone to great lengths.

I did go to great lengths, both in Ireland and in Spain and France."

"My point precisely." Though Weston, who knew so much, didn't know Raoul had actually been working against the British in Spain and France.

"You trusted me enough to come to me, Algy. If I'm to help you, you need to continue to trust me."

Weston turned to the windows for a moment, then turned back to Raoul. His shoulders were still a taut line, but he seemed to have surrendered something within him. "Rannoch seduced Anne. She made every sort of excuse for him, but it was plain to me he took advantage of a young bride with no town polish. The games his set indulged in were bad enough, but to take advantage of a girl like that, and to do it for a wager—" He turned away again. His hands had curled into fists at his sides.

"Believe me, I can understand the impulse," Raoul said. "For all I abhor dueling."

Weston met his gaze for a moment. "I confess part of me wanted to smash something. Had wanted to do so ever since Anne broke with me. For the sake of her family. For reasons I could do nothing but nod to with understanding. And make myself scarce to make it easier on her."

"And then she needed you again."

"Yes. Or I thought she did. She was furious about the duel. But I couldn't bring myself to pull back. Or I didn't want to. I told myself Rannoch would do the same to other young women. Which I have no doubt was true, though I can't argue our duel stopped him. We did avoid open scandal, but the risk to Anne was foolish."

"Hugh Cresswell was your second."

"Yes, it was good of him. We were at Cambridge together, though I hadn't seen much of him in years. The night I challenged Alistair Rannoch—at White's, where I didn't dare show my face for years after—he happened to be coming out of the card room when I threw down my glove. He at once offered to support me. Which was a fortunate thing, as it had just dawned on me then that I could hardly take someone else into my confidence to act for me without betraying Anne's secrets. He managed the whole thing very creditably. By the time of the duel, I'd got past the impulse to end Rannoch's miserable life. Perhaps I've never believed the cause was worth anything as you did, even when the cause was Anne's honor."

"And perhaps you aren't a cold-blooded killer, and recognized what the scandal would do to Lady Darlington."

"Perhaps. I didn't act well. I didn't act enough with Anne's interests at heart. But I still fail to see what that has to do with the situation now."

Raoul drew a breath. For all he prided himself on weighing things in advance, confiding secrets and damaging someone's view of their friends and actions still brought him up short. "Hugh Cresswell was at Lady Darlington's ball where the letters most likely disappeared."

Weston stared at Raoul, not with anger, but as though Raoul had taken leave of his senses. "Yes, of course he was. Along with more than fifty other people."

"Yes, but Cresswell knew about your relationship with Lady Darlington. Did he know about the letters?"

"No. That is—" Weston scowled at Fanny's lilac satin curtains. "Christ, I can't be sure what I told him. It was almost two decades ago, and I was hardly in a settled frame of mind. The fact that I'd written letters to Anne would hardly have seemed such a great secret."

"Did he know what was in the letters?"

"You mean that I was working with the United Irishmen? No. Even blinded by love and anger I wasn't a complete fool. I wouldn't have confided that." Weston studied Raoul. "Why so much suspicion of Cresswell?"

Raoul met his friend's gaze. "Cresswell is in a club of sorts. Called the Elsinore League. Have you heard of it?"

"No. Is it a theatrical society? He never struck me as the sort for that."

"No. It's anything but. Alistair Rannoch was one of the founding members. So was Lord Beverston, with whom he had the wager over Lady Darlington and who was his second in the duel."

"Christ. Are you suggesting Cresswell was part of it? That the whole thing was orchestrated?"

"Not necessarily. But the fact that Cresswell conveniently appeared in time to be your second is suggestive. And the League are known to employ blackmail."

"Why? What the devil did they want from me then? Why would they want me to resign now?"

"I can't answer that. Not yet."

"Perhaps because there isn't an answer. Perhaps because your whole theory is false."

"Perhaps. When did you last see Cresswell?"

Weston frowned. "At White's a few weeks ago. We did little more than exchange nods. He's a decent fellow, but we move in different circles. And after the duel, I confess I didn't want reminding of the incident. You won't—"

"I'll take care we don't reveal to him anything he doesn't know already."

"Thank you. I know it must be difficult to do this with your wedding in scarcely a week."

"The wedding means a great deal, but it hardly absorbs all my energies. Or Laura's." Raoul hesitated a moment. "Algy—I've always prided myself on not being the sort who inquires into a friend's personal life. But your feelings for Lady Darlington do not seem to have dimmed. You're both free now—"

Weston gave a twisted smile. "Imagining happy endings for

everyone because you finally got one yourself? We're not all so fortunate, my friend."

"It seems rather sad to call marriage an ending, and I'd never be fool enough to claim one sort of happiness resolves all the challenges in life. But I am rather keenly aware now of the value of reaching for happiness when one can."

"Anne and I aren't starry-eyed young lovers any more."

"No, you're adults with more experience of life, probably better suited to build a stable future."

"My dear fellow, you talk as if we could ignore our past."

"I don't think anyone can do that. The trick is to find a way to build on it."

Weston gave another smile, a bit less bitter but still as though he were imagining something out of reach. "You're a good fellow, O'Roarke."

Raoul clapped his friend on the shoulder. "You were willing to take risks once, Algy. We all grow more cautious with time, even me. But sometimes a risk can be worth it."

$\mathcal{M}$alcolm released his breath at the gleam of his sister's hair in the shadows.

Gisèle turned her head and met his gaze with a smile. She was sitting at a gateleg table in the empty cottage on the edge of London, where they had agreed to meet. "You look surprised. Did you think I wouldn't come?"

"No. But I'm relieved to see you safe."

"Oh, Malcolm. You don't trust me."

Malcolm advanced into the room. There was dust on the floor, but a handsome Turkey rug covered the floorboards. "I trust you as I trust few people, sister mine. I have the same fears about Mel or Raoul or Harry. And they're the best agents I know. You may be among their number."

"High praise." Gisèle tilted her head back to look up at him. "I'm not doing anything like going behind enemy lines."

"Aren't you?" Malcolm hooked a chair with his foot and dropped down across from her.

"Not in the midst of a war."

"That depends on one's definition of a war. No one saw you?"

"I know how to lay a false trail. And to double back. I shouldn't stay long, though."

"Whose cottage is this?"

"People Julien knows. They're abroad. You needn't worry."

Julien St. Juste was a number of things, but he was undeniably a first-class agent, and Malcolm had come to believe he had Gisèle's interests at heart. Malcolm fixed his sister with a hard stare across the table. Her cheekbones were more pronounced than the last time he'd seen her. The set of her shoulders betrayed the whipcord strength of one honing her skills. But her hands were steady on the table, her gaze level and contained. She was sipping a glass of whisky. Sipping, not drinking quickly. She picked up the bottle and poured a glass for him.

Malcolm took a sip. "What have you learned, Gelly?"

Gisèle leaned forwards, hands curved round her glass. "Lord Weston. You've guessed the League are behind the blackmail?"

"We wondered. Why do they want to get rid of him?"

"He wants to appoint Jasper Fitzsimmons as a junior secretary."

Malcolm clunked his glass down in surprise. He had a vague image of Fitzsimmons, five or so years younger than Malcolm himself, from a prominent Tory family, now a young MP who had earned his first seat in Parliament in the recent election. "What do the League have against Fitzsimmons?"

"I don't think it's what they have against Fitzsimmons. I think it's who they want in the position in his place."

"Who?"

"Alexander Trenor."

Malcolm stared at his sister. *"Sandy?"*

"You're friends with him, aren't you?"

"Yes. He's a good lad. He's also seemingly quite without ambition. His father isn't a League member. Why the devil do they want him in a position of power?"

Gisèle shook her head. "I don't know. I got Tommy to tell me it was because they want Sandy to have the job by feigning complete disbelief in their targeting Weston. Then I asked why they'd care about Fitzsimmons. Tommy admitted they want Sandy Trenor to have the post, but he couldn't or wouldn't say more. Could Sandy Trenor really be some sort of agent?"

"I find that very hard to believe." And yet, Bet's comments about Sandy's being disturbed and his own sense that Sandy was play-acting echoed in his mind. "That said, a number of people have surprised me. Including the person presently sitting across from me. But even before you ran from Dunmykel, even before I had a clue as to your true abilities, I'd have said you had the makings of an agent much more than Sandy appears to."

Gisèle titled her head to one side. "Truly?"

"Truly."

"Thank you."

"It's the truth." Malcolm took a sip of whisky. "Who took the papers?"

"I'm not sure. Nor where they have them hidden. Not yet."

"Go carefully. We should be able to resolve this."

"It's more important than it seems, Malcolm."

"It's a man's life. Or at least work and reputation and the life he's built. Not to mention the life and reputation of the woman he once loved."

"That, yes. But I'm sure it's also part of something bigger. As it so often is with the League."

Malcolm nodded. Only a few minutes more and so much he needed to know, for reasons both practical and emotional. "How are you, Gelly?"

"I told you last time. I'm managing."

He studied the lines round her eyes, lines that hadn't been there a year ago, in the light of the coal oil lamp. Though they had a communication system, he was careful not to ask precisely where she was. "You're back in England. You don't have to answer, but you must be to have been able to meet me so quickly."

She hesitated a moment, turning her glass in her ha. "Tommy needed to meet with Beverston and some others in person. I'm staying with him in the country. I know you won't ask me where."

Malcolm continued to watch her, the face of a hardened agent overlaid over the face of the little sister whose scraped knees he'd bandaged and kissed. There was no such easy cure for the scrapes and bruises she was acquiring now. "It can weigh on one. As time goes on. You have to live in the moment. Let yourself forget at times that you're playing a role."

"So now you want me to do this?"

"For the moment I need to think like a spymaster, not a brother. As a spymaster, as a fellow agent, I'm telling you you need to do whatever you can to stay in your role. Including letting yourself escape into it. It's the only way to survive. I don't know how Mel did it all those years."

"I'm not lying to the person I love."

Questions about his sister's relationship to Tommy Belmont shot through his mind. Questions he had no right to ask. "Yes, well, in Mel's case my feelings for her probably helped keep me from seeing the truth. Almost certainly did."

"But she had to contend with your brilliance. The League are good. But I don't think any are your equal."

"No need to exaggerate."

"I'm not. I'm being scrupulously honest about how I see it." Gisèle twisted the glass again, watching the shadows cast by the lamp. "It's easier now I have Ian with me. He keeps me in the moment."

Gisèle had left her baby son with her husband when she first ran off to work with the League. But Andrew was engaged in dangerous work himself now and they'd agreed Ian was safer with Gisèle, for a number of reasons. The risk still made Malcolm grow cold at times but Gisèle had pointed out that having her child with her would convince the League she was in earnest in

hem. And he counted on her child's presence to
) some sense of the risks she was running. At least
d it would. "You saw Andrew."

ı. I told the League I had to take Ian to see him as
part of my cover. It was—" She drew a breath, scraping through
the possibilities for the right word. "Hard. And wonderful." She
swallowed the last of her whisky. "Julien taught me early on that
one of the first rules of pulling off a successful mission is not to
get distracted and take too long meeting with one's contact." She
pushed back her chair and got to her feet.

Malcolm stood as well. The instinct to hug her warred with
the spymaster's advice he had just given.

Gisèle gave a sudden smile, closed the distance between them,
and kissed his cheek. "I love you, Malcolm. I'll even risk stepping
out of character to say so."

GISÈLE LINGERED IN THE SHADOWS OUTSIDE THE COTTAGE, MAKING
sure she sensed no one watching. Or that Malcolm, who was
supposed to be waiting inside to let her get away first, hadn't
decided to follow her. Or didn't have Mélanie or Raoul or Harry
waiting to follow her. Not that she thought they would. Not at
this point. Too much risk to everyone. And if they'd made up their
minds to bring her in, they could have just tried to snatch her
from the cottage. Besides, they seemed to value her intelligence.
And to respect her right to make her own decisions.

She made her way through the shadows, by a deliberately
meandering route different from the one she had taken to get
there. Not hurrying, pausing every now and then to breathe in the
night air and take stock of her surroundings. They were on the
edge of London but she could smell cows and chickens, and as the
wind shifted, a whiff of a vegetable garden that bought a sudden,
sharp memory of Dunmykel, a stab beneath her breastbone.

She turned a corner, skirting a heap of refuse, and felt her senses prickle. Then she let out a sigh of relief as a dark figure detached itself from the shadows and fell into step beside her. "I could have made it back perfectly well on my own," she said.

"I have no doubt of it," Julien St. Juste returned. "Extra insurance. If by any chance the League are aware of anything—which I doubt they will be—they'll think you were meeting me, not Malcolm."

"And that's better?"

"Given their view of me, it would make you less of a traitor in their eyes." She felt his gaze run over her in the dark. "You told him?"

"What I could. Obviously he can't know all of it."

"Challenging."

"If they can save Weston, it will help."

"It will certainly help Weston. And yes, it will at least slow things. We could use the time."

Gisèle felt the pressure of her brother's arms round her when she'd kissed him goodbye. "I hate lying to Malcolm."

"I think you're proud you can pull it off."

She shot a look at him. His eyes gleamed like a knife blade in the dark. "Maybe a bit. Oh, all right, yes, I am. Mostly I can't quite believe I can do it. But it doesn't stop me from feeling guilty." She folded her arms over her chest "He can't know the truth. It would destroy him."

"He's going to have to some day."

A chill shot through her. She saw herself as hardened, but there were some things she still couldn't contemplate. "Not until we've made things safe."

"That's rather a tall order."

"Then why are we doing all this?"

Julien grabbed her arm and pulled her against the wall of a house as someone emptied a chamber pot from an upper story window. "I said it was a tall order, not that we couldn't accomplish it." He looked down at her in the faint glow of moonlight and pushed a strand of hair behind her ear. "Malcolm's very good at what he does. So are Mélanie and O'Roarke and Harry and Archie Davenport. Not to mention Cordelia and Laura Tarrington and Lady Frances. Even without all the information, I'd lay odds they'll save Weston. We can worry about the rest of it."

CHAPTER 7

"How on earth would Sandy's being in office help the League?" Cordelia demanded.

Despite the late hour, they were all in the Berkeley Square library. In fact, the two Davenport couples and their children were spending the night at the Rannochs', Frances having declared that though she might not have been as attentive a parent as she should, there was no way she'd be able to sleep before she had a report on Gisèle. The older children were asleep upstairs under Blanca's watch. Frances and Archie were holding the babies, and Jessica was asleep in Mélanie's lap as Drusilla was in Cordy's. At times like this Mélanie was grateful they had such a large London house.

"I've been asking myself that ever since Gelly told me." Malcolm took a swallow of the coffee Mélanie had been keeping everyone supplied with. Mélanie could see the weight of his interview with his sister in his gaze. "Unless my instincts are truly off, and Sandy's the cleverest Elsinore League agent I've ever encountered, they see some gain from his being in the position."

"Easy to manipulate?" Frances suggested. "He's an endearing young man, and he's certainly grown up in the past months, but I

e League thinking they could bend him to

le theory," Malcolm said. "But leaves the question ɜue think they can get from having someone they can control as a junior secretary in the Duchy of Lancaster."

"Could we be wrong about Marchmain?" Raoul asked Archie. "Could he actually be an Elsinore League member?"

Archie frowned. "It's possible. If so, I would think anyone about whom there was so much secrecy would be very high up in the League indeed. Which I suppose could explain Marchmain's pull."

"And this is all just to get his son a promotion?" Cordelia asked.

"It seems odd he wouldn't have done the same for Matthew if that were the case, though," Harry said.

"I'll talk to Roger Smythe," Malcolm said. "I saw him today and he said he'd look into the duel. I'll see if he got wind of anything about Sandy as well." Lord Beverston's younger son Roger had become an ally in their investigation last winter, though he was hardly on comfortable terms with his father. He hesitated a moment. "And I should probably talk to Carfax."

"Fortitude, old man," Harry murmured.

Malcolm grinned at him. "Even I'll admit he deserves a report on Gisèle. And he should know if the League are trying to control government appointments. But I'll need to do it without giving him a whiff of the truth about Weston." He glanced at Raoul.

"I have every faith in you, Malcolm," Raoul said.

Malcolm gave a wry grin. "I only wish I could say the same about myself."

≈

MALCOLM MOVED TO THE CRADLE, THE SLEEPING JESSICA DRAPED over his shoulder. "Aunt Frances was remarkably restrained. Barely a question about Gelly."

"I think it was enough for her to hear you say Gisèle was well." Mélanie closed the door to the night nursery. The older children were all asleep, along with Berowne and Chloe's dog, though Mélanie had told Malcolm there'd been excited whispers the first two times she'd gone to check on them. "She was white-knuckled while you were gone."

Malcolm settled Jessica in the cradle and eased his hands out from under her. "I'll own I breathe easier every time I see Gelly." He drew the covers over their daughter. "She did look well. At least as well as one might expect. She's lost weight."

"It can be hard to eat undercover." Mélanie was standing still beside her dressing table, watching him.

Malcolm ran his fingers over their daughter's hair, then turned back to face his wife. "I told her to live in the moment as much as she could. I told her that was what I thought you did."

"You were right."

The delicate silver gray of Mélanie's gown fell about her in soft folds. She looked at once heartbreakingly fragile and terrifyingly strong, like finely wrought metal. Malcolm went to her side and ran his fingers down her arm. "As well as I know you, as well as I know just how brilliant you are, I don't know how you did it."

She tilted her head back, dark curls spilling over her shoulder, gaze steady on his face. "I kept my life in different boxes. I learned to smile and sip champagne even when I felt they were about to tumble down about my ears. Especially when I felt they were about to tumble down about my ears."

He slid his fingers into her own. "Would you have known if they tumbled?"

"If I was about to be caught? You caught me, so obviously not."

"If you were at the point where you couldn't keep it up any longer."

Her fingers tightened round his own, but her gaze stayed steady and thoughtful on his face. "I'd like to think I would have done. But I can't really be sure. Do you think Gisèle's at the breaking point?"

"No. If I did I'd pull her out. And I'd like to think I'd know the signs if she was . But I can't be sure."

"She's tough, Malcolm."

"I'm trying to give her the tools she needs to cope. I don't know how well equipped I am to do so."

"You've done it yourself."

"Not for this long. She has talents I don't possess. So do you."

"I had you. That made it easier and harder. I could lose myself in what we had. But I also had the guilt of lying to people I cared about."

Malcolm tightened his fingers over her own. "I wonder how different it is."

Mélanie fixed him with a level gaze. "Darling, whatever Gelly may feel for Tommy Belmont, whatever's between them, I'd stake my life it's not what I feel for you."

"No, I don't think so either." He lifted his free hand and brushed her cropped curls back from her temple. "But I also don't know that one can stay undercover successfully for a prolonged amount of time without developing some feelings for the people one is deceiving."

Her winged brows drew together. "It's a good point. I know Harry's talked about making friends undercover. Perhaps one can't avoid it unless one is totally without conscience. Like Julien."

"Quite. And I begin to wonder just how without conscience St. Juste really is."

"You're perceptive, Malcolm."

"I hope to God I am. Otherwise I've trusted my sister to a monster."

"You've seen through Julien where Raoul and I couldn't."

"Or St. Juste is changing."

"I think he is. Though if he was quite the man I thought he

was, I'm not sure he'd be capable of change." Her brows knotted a bit tighter. "Not that I'd precisely say I trust him."

"Nor would I. But I think he has Gelly's interests at heart. I think Carfax does as well. At least to a degree. That's partly why I'm going to talk to him tomorrow."

Mélanie's gaze shifted across his face. "Darling—"

"I'm willing to talk to Carfax, Mel. I'm willing to use him when it's helpful, fully acknowledging that he also uses us. But I wouldn't call him an ally. Given the past, I don't see how I ever could."

She caught his hand where it lingered at her temple. "You can't imagine I could either. But we're connected now. You could say he's part of the family."

Malcolm grimaced. Because his spymaster, the man they had fled Britain to escape, was also, they knew now, Gisèle's biological father. "Yes, God help us. Which in some ways makes me trust him less than ever."

CHAPTER 8

"**M**alcolm." Lord Carfax looked up from the papers strewn on the desk in his study and set down his pen. "Quite like old times."

"Nothing is like old times." Malcolm dropped into a chair beside Carfax's desk. A chair he had occasionally occupied as the schoolboy friend of Carfax's son, and more often later as Carfax's agent. A role he'd filled for far longer than he cared to admit. Far after he'd technically left the service of British intelligence. "Why would the League be targeting Lord Weston?"

Carfax's brows snapped together. "Are they targeting Weston?"

"They seem to be."

Carfax drew one paper over another on his desk. Probably something he didn't want Malcolm to see. "A decent man, Weston. He'd be in a more powerful position if he weren't. What do the League want him to do?"

"Not clear yet."

Carfax raised a brow. "All right, you don't want to tell me. Fair enough. But I could help you more if I knew."

"Information is to be shared judiciously. You taught me that."

"I thought O'Roarke would have done."

"Him too."

Carfax reached for another sheet of paper and added it to the other two. "You've had a report from Gisèle."

Carfax saw the United Irishmen as a threat to the stability of Britain. His learning the truth about Weston would hardly help the situation. "It can't be a surprise that I get reports from her. She thinks they're targeting Weston over whom they want appointed to a junior secretaryship in the Duchy of Lancaster."

Carfax's brows snapped together. "Why the devil would that matter to them?"

"Precisely my question. Gelly doesn't know."

"It's hardly a powerful position. Or one with access. Don't give much thought myself to who occupies it. Whom do they want in the position?"

Malcolm wasn't quite ready to share that, partly for Sandy's sake. "I don't know."

"Hmph." Carfax's gaze said he knew perfectly well Malcolm was holding something back. "How's Gisèle?"

Four months ago, Carfax had asked Malcolm about his son David in just that casual tone. It hadn't been a casual question then either.

"She's tough. Obviously under strain but shows no sign of breaking or even being close to it. I don't think I could do what she's doing. I'm trying to help her have the skills to get through it."

"Empathy gets in the way of managing agents, Malcolm."

"Putting oneself in another's shoes can be extremely useful for a spy. Or a spymaster. Or a human being."

Carfax gave a short laugh. But his brows drew together. "You still think they aren't on to her?"

"Not from what I can tell."

"What you can—"

"I can still read a situation well, sir. And she's very capable of taking care of herself."

"She's a girl of twenty."

"She's a young woman. Who was trained by one of your most capable agents."

Carfax snorted. "I take no claim for Julien."

"I can't say I trust him, but I recognize he has formidable abilities. And I think he's genuinely fond of Gisèle."

"Yes, so do I." Carfax twisted a pen between his fingers. "I can't forgive him for dragging her into the game, but I'd be far less sanguine if he weren't there to keep an eye on her." He hesitated a moment.

"I'm quite sure they aren't lovers," Malcolm said. Which was more than he could say of his sister and Tommy Belmont. "They seem to trust each other. Mel says she's never seen St. Juste trust someone so much."

Carfax's fingers clamped round the pen. "Does St. Juste know about this Weston business?"

"Gelly didn't say, but I'd imagine she's told him."

Carfax stared at the nib of the pen. "You don't think—"

"That St. Juste has actually joined the League or is playing us off against each other? No, I think St. Juste is too independent to let them use him."

"People use each other in the spy game. St. Juste knows that."

"Granted. But I don't think he'd make an alliance with the League. Because he doesn't want to be their tool. And also because I think he's too fond of my wife."

Carfax raised a brow. "Interesting."

"You aren't surprised he could be fond of someone?"

"My dear Malcolm, we're all susceptible to feeling. Even Julien. If he's fond of Mélanie, that could be useful."

Malcolm regarded his spymaster, wondering if he'd overplayed his hand. He wondered what St. Juste had said to Carfax about Mélanie. On the whole, he thought he'd prefer not to know.

"You're a sanguine husband," Carfax said.

"I said he was fond of her, not that she was of him. Actually, I think she is, to a degree. But not in the same way."

"Does he confide in her?"

Malcolm leaned back in his chair. "Do you think St. Juste confides in anyone? Though if he does, it's probably Gisèle."

Something flickered in Carfax's gaze.

"Do you know who he is?" Malcolm asked, not really expecting an answer. "Who he really is?"

"I doubt anyone knows who Julien St. Juste really is." Carfax's face remained impassive, but Malcolm could read his spymaster enough to know he was keeping it that way with an effort.

Malcolm pushed back his chair. "I understand you're coming to the wedding?

"Mélanie invited us."

"I actually think O'Roarke asked her to invite you. He's grateful for your assistance with his divorce. As we all are, of course."

"I'm glad it worked out. Amelia is looking forward to seeing you. We don't see you about as much as we use to."

"We learned to enjoy a quieter life in Italy. And we've been endeavoring to put our lives back together."

"Yes." Carfax released his breath. "I understand something about that."

Malcolm felt his fingers relax slightly against the arms of his chair. "Bel seems under the impression you and Lady Carfax are well."

"Bel doesn't know the whole story. But yes, Amelia and I are muddling through. We're not children. Amelia's always been an understanding wife." Somewhere in the crisp words was an edge of anger. In the right circumstances, even Carfax wasn't immune to guilt. And perhaps an echo of loss.

"One doesn't forget," Malcolm said. "But with time one remembers differently. And then suddenly one looks at one's spouse and realizes the shadows aren't there."

Carfax's gaze shot to his across the desk and held. "You're an extraordinarily forgiving man, Malcolm."

"I'm not sure it's about forgiveness. I think it's about understanding, to a degree. But ultimately I think it's about realizing that whatever the past, one wants a future."

"I suppose then the question, as I can imagine your saying, is what one wants that future to be?"

"I can't imagine Lady Carfax wanting any future that didn't involve you, sir."

"Failure of imagination isn't usually your difficulty, Malcolm. But anyone can suffer from it. Particularly when one has a tendency towards optimism."

"I refuse to admit to having anything of the sort. But you have been known to say I'm a good judge of people."

"Yes, I have." Carfax aligned the papers on his desktop, matching the corners with care. "Amelia isn't the sort to think of any future outside marriage. That doesn't mean she sees herself finding happiness within the marriage. It's my lookout, as I imagine you'd say of yourself. And probably less than I deserve in your eyes, for any number of actions."

"I'd never say anyone deserves unhappiness, sir."

Carfax gave a wry smile. "I suppose you'd say that's the difference between us."

Malcolm settled back in his chair and crossed his legs. "Yes, among other things."

Carfax gave what might have been called a snort. "I have nothing against happiness, but too much worrying about people's happiness can lead to all sorts of unrest." He reached for his pen. "I trust you're happier now."

"I wouldn't say I was unhappy in Italy. Quite the reverse, in fact. But yes, I'm happy to be back. More to the point, I think Mel's happy, which I was worried about."

"You're both agents, Malcolm. You're not going to be happy too far away from that life. O'Roarke understands that. He's going to find it a challenge going forwards with the life he's chosen."

"Yes, I expect he will. But if anyone understands challenges, he does. And as long as the Elsinore League are about, I don't think any one of us is going to stop being an agent."

Carfax's mouth curved in a smile like brittle parchment. "My offer still stands."

"Thank you, sir. We're well aware of it."

"And have the Elsinore League papers better guarded than the crown jewels, I don't doubt. Just don't let your feelings about me blind you to practicalities."

Malcolm got to his feet and moved to the door. "My dear sir. I don't think there's much left that I'm blind to when it comes to you."

ROGER SMYTHE LOOKED ACROSS THE ROLLING GRASS OF GREEN Park at his three-year-old daughter Marina playing an enthusiastic game of tag with Colin, Jessica, and Emily. "So much easier for children. They can just play without wasting time trying to sort things out."

"Very true," Malcolm said. "Except when they suddenly decide they never want to see each other again. But fortunately that doesn't tend to last long."

"I think Marina notices," Roger said. "That Dorinda and I are getting on better. I never thought we let her see any constraint between us, but I think she picked up on some of it somehow."

"Children do," Malcolm said.

"It feels wrong sometimes," Roger said. "Knowing the truth about Miranda, knowing what happened to her, living with regrets, asking endless questions about what we could have done differently. It feels wrong, with all of that, to still be so happy."

"Don't ever feel guilty about being happy," Malcolm said. "It's hard enough to snatch any of it."

Roger gave a faint smile. "I think Dorinda and I are both too keenly aware of what we have to not snatch it up." He watched the children a moment longer, then said, "I need hardly tell you I'm not the best source of information on my father these days. I was as shocked as you to learn of this duel, as I told you yesterday. But my nurse's sister, Sally, was a housemaid in our household twenty years ago when the duel took place. She was friendly with Father's valet. Quite friendly, I think, though as a child one doesn't understand those things. She's retired from service now, married to a man who has a public house in Hampstead. I went to visit her yesterday after I spoke with you. I take Marina to see her regularly, so even if Father's having me followed, it won't necessarily clue him in to anything. Sally said Thornton, Father's valet, told her about the duel at the time. Made a great fuss about the need to be quiet and how he was sharing important secrets. He said Hugh Cresswell came to see Father the night before the duel."

"That's not necessarily surprising. As seconds they might have had details to discuss. Or even been trying to patch things up."

"Yes, that was my thought as well. But Sally said Thornton told her he heard them laughing together. Almost as though they were part of some shared joke—her words, quoting Thornton. And that Thornton said he was sure there was something rum going on. Sally said he actually seemed worried."

"Dueling's bad enough. But if a duel's orchestrated, it can be close to murder."

Roger nodded. He had few illusions when it came to his father, Malcolm knew. "So you think that's it? Father and Alistair Rannoch and Hugh Cresswell set out to entrap Lord Weston?"

"It looks more and more that way. We still don't know why. All right, Jessica?" Malcolm called as his daughter stumbled.

Jessica nodded and waved as she scrambled to her feet.

"Have you ever heard your father talk about Sandy Trenor?" Malcolm asked Roger, gaze still on the children.

"Sandy?" Roger said on the same note of surprise Malcolm had heard in his own voice at Gisèle's revelation. "Surely you don't think he was working for Father alongside Matt?"

"It is hard to credit." Malcolm looked at his own son and had a memory of Sandy wrestling with Colin on the Berkeley Square drawing room carpet. "I don't have any reason to think he did. But apparently the League are targeting Weston because they want Sandy given a junior secretaryship in the Duchy of Lancaster."

"Good God." Roger frowned at a leafy birch tree. "The League take devious paths at times. But it's difficult to see why they would care who was appointed to the junior secretaryship, let alone want Sandy Trenor in the job."

"Yes, that's the general response from everyone I've talked to. You don't think Marchmain could secretly be a League member, do you?"

"A secret member of a secret organization?" Roger's mouth gave a wry twist. "Like you, I think there are members whose names aren't on the list you obtained. But I have no reason to think Marchmain is among their number. You think he could be behind this and doing all of it simply to help his son to an office? And the others are helping him simply out of fellow feeling?"

"League members do favors for each other. More as a quid pro quo than out of fellow feeling, I think. Or they might see Sandy as someone they could manipulate."

"To do what?"

"That remains the question. I suppose if they're playing a long game they could see this as setting him up on a career that would eventually take him somewhere useful to them."

"A lot of 'ifs' in that."

"Yes. Including that Sandy has far more mettle than they're allowing for. If that is their motivation."

"Father was willing to use John," Roger said, "more than he seems to have been scheming for his advancement. And my views are too different from his for him even to have tried with me. But all the League may not be the same in that regard. Have you asked Sandy?"

"No. It would be too much of a burden for him to keep the secret, especially if his father's involved." Malcolm pictured Sandy in Piccadilly, giving a carefully crafted performance of young man about town. "And if, by any chance, I'm wrong about him, it could be ruinous for him to know what we know."

CHAPTER 9

eston stared at Raoul. "Alexander Trenor? Marchmain's youngest? He's barely down from Oxford."

"He's been down a year or two, but yes," Raoul said. "And that's more or less everyone's response."

"*That's* what all this is about?" Weston said.

"It seems to be part of it, at least."

Weston frowned. "Someone did mention Trenor to me in connection with the position. Cooperthwaite, I think. Yes, it was definitely he. I said the job needed someone with a bit more experience, and I was quite set on Jasper Fitzsimmons. He wasn't the first person to suggest someone for the post, so I didn't think much of it. That set them looking for information on me?"

"We're obviously missing pieces of the puzzle. But we're getting closer. Trust us a bit longer, Algy."

"I've trusted you with my life in the past, O'Roarke. I don't have much choice but to do so again now."

Raoul saw Weston out of Frances and Archie's house through the mews. Archie was out making inquiries of his own, but Fanny was in her sitting room with Chloe and the babies. Raoul stopped to drink a cup of tea with them, wrestle on the hearth rug with Chloe's dog, and hold both Francesca and Philip. They were growing by the day, seemingly, but both still fit in the curve of his forearm.

"You look very natural," Frances said.

"I'm a good actor," he reminded her.

He left the house shortly after for the brief walk to Berkeley Square, his mind filled with images of a future that had once seemed impossible. The baby would be here in little more than a month. He knew a lot more than when he'd anticipated Malcolm's birth with a mixture of joy and trepidation. Enough to be at once reassured and even more alarmed. He'd never anticipated sitting beside the woman he loved when she gave birth. And if a part of his mind wondered what was happening in Spain, questioned if he'd left sufficient instructions for his agents there, he knew beyond a doubt where he needed to be. Not to mention where he wanted to be.

He felt himself smile as he turned down an alley to cut through to Berkeley Street. Picturing Laura's face. Which was probably why he caught the flash of movement to his right a split second too late. Two men rushed him. He dodged to the side, but one caught him a glancing blow that sent him spinning against the rough boards of the building opposite.

He spun to the side as the other man charged at him. His coat caught on the splintery wood and jerked him back. The fabric tore as he wrenched away. He grabbed a loose board and hit the first attacker over the head. The second man grabbed his shoulder from behind. His coat tore again, this time as he whirled away from a knife. He spun round and pinned the first man in a flying tackle. The second man lunged for him. He braced for impact, but the second man went flying across the alley.

The first man scrambled to his feet and the two men darted off.

Raoul found himself looking up at a familiar pair of mocking blue eyes. "Thank you, St. Juste." Raoul sprang to his feet. "I seem to be saying that uncomfortably often, of late."

Julien St. Juste smoothed his coat sleeve. "Alliances have shifted a bit. One finds oneself depending more on some people. Besides, you need to stay alive for pretty Laura Tarrington. And because I'm quite intrigued to see you as a married man."

Raoul brushed off his coat. "I've been a married man since before I met you, Julien."

"Marriage is more than a bit of paper. Or at least I assume that's what you'd say. And the Rannochs and the Davenports—both pairs of them—and the rest of you who seem to take it so seriously."

"True enough. What are you doing here, Julien?"

"Saving you, it seems. And giving you some information about the Weston situation. Malcolm talked to Gisèle," he added.

"Yes, I know. What—"

"Better I tell all of you, I think. I can slip into the house undetected."

"Don't remind me."

"We're allies, remember."

"Colleagues. Are you coming to the wedding?"

Julien raised a brow.

"I wouldn't mind having a friend there."

"You have lots of friends now. An indecent number, I would say. Positively domestic of you. One wonders if you've forgot to be on your guard."

"I mean, a friend from my old life."

Julien frowned in consideration. "Interesting. I suppose I might feel the same were I ever in your shoes, which I can't really imagine. You aren't going to ask me to stand up with you, are you?"

"No, Malcolm is."

"Of course he is. Will the Carfaxes be there?"

"Probably. Is that a problem?"

"On the contrary. It will be quite amusing. By all means, I'll attend."

"THAT WASN'T A RANDOM ATTACK, BY RIVAL SMUGGLERS OR otherwise," Malcolm said. Mélanie had felt the tension rising off him ever since Raoul came into the house, torn coat and scraped face giving the lie to his nonchalance.

"No," Raoul conceded. "I'll admit that. It still didn't seem as well orchestrated as what the League could pull off if they were really serious, but I was fortunate to have St. Juste show up, just as I was fortunate to have you come to my aid at the docks."

Laura slid her hand into his own. Her gaze was steady, but her skin was more than usually pale. "I hate to seem a worrier, but I don't want to be your widow before I've had a chance to be your wife."

Raoul pressed a kiss to her temple. "It won't come to that, sweetheart. But I would like to know why the League are acting now. And acting rather ineptly, at that."

"A way to put us on edge, perhaps," Archie said.

"In which case, it's working," Frances said. She and Archie, returned from his own inquiries, had walked round to Berkeley Square shortly after Raoul returned.

"Surely they don't think this would stop us from trying to retrieve Lord Weston's letters?" Cordelia said.

"No," Malcolm said, "but they may think if we're distracted we'll be less efficient."

"The whole thing could be a distraction," Harry said.

"Blackmailing Weston to set us searching for the letters and distract us from whatever they're doing?" Malcolm said. "In which case they're deliberately feeding us false information through Gelly."

"Not necessarily," Harry said. "I tend to think she'd know if they were on to her. They may well genuinely want to get rid of Weston. But perhaps that's not their main focus. Perhaps only a few members know what the real focus is."

"And the League don't always act in concert," Archie pointed out. "It's entirely possible there's more than one plan underway with different members not knowing what the other is doing. Or that one faction is using the Weston plot and attacking Raoul as a distraction."

"Yes," Mélanie said, "but then—"

She broke off as a draft cut through the room and the bronze velvet curtains stirred. "Greetings, friends and enemies. Or are we all friends now?" Julien dropped down from the windowsill.

"You'd have made a better entrance if you hadn't told Raoul you were coming," Mélanie said. "Not that we don't all appreciate your coming to his assistance."

Julien unfolded himself like a cat getting up from a leisurely nap. "I expect O'Roarke could have handled them perfectly well on his own."

"Flattering, Julien," Raoul said.

"No, it's the truth. I don't have any need to flatter you just now, O'Roarke. Or any illusions that flattery would work. Just as well you got out of it before you got any more roughed up, though. Wouldn't want to have your pretty face marred for the wedding. My felicitations, Lady Tarrington. I hope you know what you're getting into."

"Thank you, Mr. St. Juste." Laura smiled at him. "I do. If I didn't, I'd be worried I'd be bored."

Julien flung his head back and gave a laugh of genuine appreciation. "That's one thing I don't think anyone in this room will be. Not for the foreseeable future. Might I have a glass of that whisky? I've had rather an eventful day."

Malcolm moved to the drinks trolley with an amused smile and poured a glass of whisky.

"Out with it, Julien," Mélanie said. "What have you learned?"

Julien dropped into a straight-backed chair. "It was Hugh Cresswell's valet's afternoon off. I had a few pints with him at the Lazy Dog in Piccadilly. Thank you, Rannoch." He took the glass of whisky Malcolm was holding out to him. "It seems the night of Lady Darlington's ball, Cresswell dismissed his valet and said he'd undress himself. Apparently unheard of."

"So he did take the letters," Raoul said. "Poor Weston."

"And the letters are probably in his room." Malcolm returned to his seat on the sofa beside Mélanie.

"The Cresswells are giving a ball tomorrow night," Cordelia said. "We were invited."

"So were we," Mélanie said. "I politely declined. If Malcolm and I attend, Cresswell is sure to guess we're after the papers. If they know Weston was involved with the United Irishmen, they know he knows Raoul. They could guess he'd come to us, even if they aren't actually having him followed. We might have got away with it when we went about in society more, but the way we've been living, our suddenly showing up at a society event we had at first declined would be a dead giveaway."

"I could get them for you," Julien suggested.

"Thank you, St. Juste, we can handle this ourselves." Malcolm met Mélanie's gaze across the sofa. "We just won't go as ourselves."

Mélanie grinned. What was it about a mission in disguise that made her feel such delight? "They'll have to have hired footmen on for the evening."

"My thinking exactly," Malcolm said. "It's too long since I've seen you in breeches." He looked at Harry and Cordelia. "You should accept the invitation."

"But they're bound to suspect us as well," Cordelia said.

"Exactly. Cresswell will be busy watching you and not worrying about what a couple of stray footmen are doing. And you'll be there as backup if Mel and I need it."

Cordelia grinned. Harry gave a sardonic smile. "I never did much care for being a decoy."

Cordelia curled her hand round his arm. "Not even when you can dance with me?"

"Well, there are compensations."

"We're going to cause a bit of a stir showing up as well," Cordelia said. "I rather like causing a stir again. Of the right sort."

Frances's brows drew together. "We were invited as well. We could —"

Malcolm shook his head. "Cresswell will be even more suspicious of Archie. Stay home with the babies. And try to keep O'Roarke from doing anything foolish." Malcolm grinned at his father.

"My dear Malcolm." Raoul settled back on the settee beside Laura. "I may still be a field agent, but I'm also a spymaster. Part of drawing up a good mission is knowing when to entrust it to someone else."

"You were very forbearing." Malcolm set down the whisky decanter after refilling his and Raoul's glasses. Julien had made himself scarce, and the Davenport couples had gone home after staying for dinner and strategizing. Mélanie and Laura had gone upstairs to check on the children. "In fact, you were so agreeable to being left out of the mission it's distinctly suspicious."

Raoul grinned as he accepted a glass of whisky from Malcolm. "My dear Malcolm. Loath as I am to admit it, I can contribute most by being ostentatiously at home to anyone who happens to be watching me. Besides, I imagine you and Mélanie will enjoy the action."

Malcolm gave a wry grin. He wasn't going to admit just how his senses quickened over the prospect of what was a relatively simple retrieval operation. "All right, a bit. All right, possibly more than a bit." He took a drink of whisky. "It's difficult to let go. Though seeing Gelly, I'm reminded how fortunate I am to be out of it for the most part." He dropped down on the sofa. "She's very matter-of-fact. No sign of cracking. But she's lost weight. Just as Mel did before Waterloo."

Raoul moved to the sofa beside him. "Yes, that was worrying."

Malcolm shot a look at his father. "Did you ever think about pulling Mel out?"

Raoul hesitated a moment. "It never got that far."

"But you must have been prepared to do so if you had to."

"I'd have been a fool and unbelievably callous if I hadn't been."

Malcolm set his glass down. "How did you know? That it wasn't that desperate? What would have told you if suddenly it were?"

His father's brows drew together, as though in honest thought. "Her brilliance never faltered. But more than that, she could laugh. She could lose herself in the moment. If she'd ever lost the ability to do that—I did ask her once. Not long before Waterloo. If it was too much. If she wanted me to get her out. Of course she didn't."

"What would you have done if she did? Or if she said she didn't, but you thought she was going to break?"

Raoul turned his glass in his hand. "Tried to do something that wouldn't destroy her cover. Like having her withdraw to Ghent as some of the other wives did, or even go to Britain. It wouldn't have been hard to fake her being ill. Or Colin. Normally, you'd have gone with them, but with battle about to break out—"

"You're right. A part of me would have been relieved to get them to safety."

Raoul nodded. "But if necessary, I'd have pulled her and Colin out without explanation." He paused a moment. "I was fairly sure you'd have figured it out and followed eventually."

Malcolm reached for his glass. "That's giving me rather a lot of credit."

"Not more than you deserve. I'm quite sure you'd have worked out the truth. And I'm fairly sure you'd have wanted your wife back."

"So am I. Though it would have been the devil of a mess for a while. Probably more so than it was later, and that was bad enough." Malcolm scanned Raoul's face, the face he could read so much better now but which still held untold secrets. "What would you have done if you'd thought I was about to work out the truth?"

Raoul was silent. His fingers curved round the crystal etched with the Rannoch crest. Not choosing his words so much as sorting through his thoughts, Malcolm thought. "I'd like to think I'd have advised her to tell you the truth. But I'm not sure. The spymaster's instincts to control information. After all, we were at war, and you were an enemy agent. I might have made sure she and Colin were on neutral ground and told you myself."

"Given that we were at war and I was an enemy agent, that would have been quite a risk too."

"But it would have been my risk to take." Raoul took a drink of whisky. "I've always protected my agents. But at this point, there's no sense in pretending that I wouldn't have gone even further to protect Mélanie and Colin. Or that I wouldn't have felt the very least I owed you was an explanation."

"Progress. You're learning."

"What?"

"To admit you have feelings."

"My dear Malcolm. I rather thought you'd worked that out some time ago."

"Which isn't the same as your admitting it."

"Yes, well, since last January I'm trying to do better with keeping secrets."

Malcolm studied his father for a long moment. "I may have to decide if we need to pull Gisèle. I don't think she'll agree with it."

"No. She's less seasoned than Mélanie was by Waterloo, and so more reckless. But she's not foolhardy."

"She's more at risk than Mel was. You have to have known I'd never move against Mel, whatever I learned."

"My dear Malcolm, I rarely say I'm sure of anything, but I'm sure of that."

"Which can't be said of Beverston or Tommy Belmont, when it comes to Gisèle."

"No. Though there are a number of reasons they'll move carefully when it comes to her. Her position. Her connections to Frances, and Frances's to the royal family. And in Belmont's case, at least a certain amount of affection. You have plans in place. We have St. Juste if the plans go awry. And there's always the option of breaking in and kidnapping her as a last resort."

"That's not funny."

"No, it's an actual suggestion."

"There's Ian too."

"She keeps Ian close. And he's a large part of what's keeping her sane, I imagine. We could snatch both of them if we had to. We have formidable resources. The two of us. Mélanie. Archie and Harry. Bertrand and Rupert. Laura and Cordelia, who wouldn't let themselves be left out. St. Juste, though I hate to admit it. We could pull it off if we had to."

Malcolm found himself laughing despite the gravity of the situation. "Damn it, yes, I think we could. I just hope to God, for a number of reasons, that we don't have to."

CHAPTER 10

$\mathcal{M}$élanie adjusted her powdered wig. Addison had found the names of two of the additional footmen hired for the evening, a pair of brothers who worked in their family's haberdashery and were making some extra money. A generous payment had persuaded them to stay home for the evening and give their livery to the Rannochs. It would be obvious to Cresswell later what had happened, but by that time it would be too late for him to do anything about it.

She was on the shorter side for a footman, but she'd added cork lifts to her silver-buckled shoes. And in hiring extra footmen for a ball, standards about such things as all being six feet tall tended to be relaxed. It was a long time since she'd masqueraded as a man, but she knew how to shift her center of gravity and deepen her voice.

"Here, take these champagne glasses." Malcolm put a tray in her hands. He was using the faintly Scottish-tinged accent he often adopted when on a mission.

Mélanie accepted the tray and made her way to the supper room. She caught a glimpse of Lady Cresswell at the head of the stairs, greeting guests, and had a memory of doing the same herself less than a year ago. The clink of glasses, the smell of hothouse roses and Parisian perfume, the brilliance of wax tapers reflected in gilt-edged mirrors were all familiar, but it was like seeing them from a different side of the footlights. Or perhaps like being a stagehand instead of an actress.

"Oh, thank goodness, champagne." A white-gloved hand encircled by a diamond bracelet snagged a glass off Mélanie's tray.

Mélanie looked up with the faint diffidence of one in an unfamiliar setting, mindful of his place, and met Cordelia's bright gaze.

"I'll take one to my husband as well. Goodness, you look realistic," Cordelia murmured as she leaned forwards to take a second glass. "You'd never guess usually you have every eye in the ballroom on you. Oh, Eugenia, darling." Cordy spun away in a swirl of ivory tulle and brushed her cheek against that of a dark-haired woman with diamonds in her hair. Mélanie let her gaze drift past Harry, standing near the archway to the ballroom, but didn't risk making eye contact.

Hugh Cresswell moved into her line of sight, a pretty blonde woman, ten years his wife's junior, on his arm. Despite his companion's attractions, she saw his gaze go to Harry. So far, so good. Their decoy was working.

The musicians in the ballroom had launched into a waltz she remembered dancing to with Malcolm before they left London. Speaking of Malcolm, there he was, lighting a taper that had gone out in one of the candelabra on the sideboard. A woman in purple and diamonds brushed past her. Lady Winchester, who had always disliked Mélanie because, Mélanie was convinced, she had wanted Malcolm for one of her own daughters. She usually managed to say something cutting about Mélanie's toilette in the guise of a compliment. Tonight she didn't even notice her. What a thing to be anonymous in a London ballroom.

A white gown with silver spangles caught her eye across the room. Worn by a slender woman with smooth pale gold hair and something indefinably French about the flick of her gloved wrist. Sylvie St. Ives was a French émigrée married to a British aristocrat. She had also been an agent of Carfax's until she broke free, as well as undertaking work for Fouché, the former French minister of police. And she had committed murder the previous June, though they hadn't been able to prove it.

Another slim, gloved hand, this one belonging to a gentleman, shot out to retrieve a champagne glass. "I forgot how good you looked in knee breeches," a familiar voice said.

His hair was darkened, his cheeks plumped out, his middle thickened, but the voice was unmistakable. Especially as he'd made no effort to disguise it. "What are you doing here, Julien?" Mélanie asked.

"Enjoying the performance," Julien St. Juste said. "And supplying additional backup if you need it. We're on the same side now, remember?"

"We have interests in common."

"What more can one ask for?" Julien was looking at her, yet she knew his gaze was taking in the entire room. She could have named a guest, even one standing behind him, and he'd have told her precisely what that person was doing. "Do you need help creating a diversion?"

"Thank you. I think we have things in hand."

"I'm here if you need me." He frowned at his glass, as though there was a spot on the rim, set it down with a grimace of distaste, and reached for another. "I suppose you've noticed Sylvie's here."

Julien had a long connection to Sylvie St. Ives. Mélanie didn't know the half of it save that they had both been Carfax's creatures, and Julien had confided in Sylvie to a surprising (for Julien) degree.

"Yes, I know. I take it you're not working with her?"

"My dear. Given recent events, surely you don't have to ask."

"I'm never sure of anything when it comes to you, Julien. Is she working tonight?"

"Sylvie's always working. I'll try to divert her. Though you're good enough to deceive her."

"No need to flatter me."

"My dear girl. As I said to O'Roarke, I don't flatter. And you don't need flattery." Julien lifted his champagne glass in a casual gesture that also managed to be a silent toast. Within twenty seconds, he vanished into the crowd.

～

"Quite like old times," Cordelia murmured, putting a champagne glass in her husband's hand.

"The ball or the mission?" Harry asked.

"Both." Cordelia smiled up at him "We're getting some very pointed looks. Being a scandal is a bit of a liability when it comes to going undetected."

"All to the good when playing decoy." Harry lifted his glass to her own.

Cordelia reached up and pressed her lips against his cheek. "Let's look the picture of domestic bliss and really give them something to gossip about."

"Goodness, it's good to see you." The Carfaxes' eldest daughter, Mary, joined them, her new husband by her side. The former Duchess of Trenchard, Mary had recently married Gui Laclos, a French émigré whom she had long loved (and who was, in fact, the father of her youngest child, born months after her husband's death). Her gaze, which had been discontented for as long as Cordelia could remember, had a glow she couldn't recall even when Mary had been the queen of the London debutantes and Cordelia had still been in the schoolroom. "Are Malcolm and Mélanie here?"

"Not tonight," Harry said in an easy voice.

"It seems nothing will coax them out. Mind you, I understand the allure of home more myself these days." She smiled up at Gui with the sort of contented bliss she once would have sneered at (for that matter, at one time Cordelia would have sneered at it herself), then turned to Cordelia. "Those are stunning earrings, Cordy."

"Thank you, they were a gift from Harry. Roman coins he found in Italy and had specially set." Cordelia smiled, conscious of a distinct relief. She and Gui had once been rather close, in the time she and Harry were apart. They were still friends and the compliment on the earrings (undeniably striking) was Mary's way of saying she didn't mind. Given the way Gui was looking at Mary (the way Gui always looked at Mary) she didn't have anything to worry about, but the comment showed an understanding not all wives had with their husband's former loves, not to mention a degree of sensitivity and kindness Cordelia wouldn't have expected from the old Mary.

"You have good taste, Colonel Davenport," Mary said.

"On occasion." Harry flashed a smile at her.

"Didn't want to come, myself," Gui murmured.

"Darling." Mary cast an affectionate glance at him. "I quite like staying home with you, but we can't do it all the time. Besides, I confess I was rather hoping to see Malcolm. Bel said he called on our father today." A flicker of concern danced through Mary's normally self-assured gaze. "I hoped—" She bit back whatever she'd been about to say and looked from Harry to Cordelia. "Is something afoot? Is that why you're here? Is it some sort of mission?"

"That's not the only reason we'd go out," Cordelia said.

"Not you, perhaps," Gui murmured, "but I doubt Davenport enjoys this sort of thing."

"It's interesting to compare London balls to Roman orgies," Harry said. "From a professional standpoint."

Mary gave an unexpected throaty laugh. "I do wish more people could hear you say so. But you're not going to distract me. I wish I could help."

"Now who's acting dissatisfied with beau monde balls?" Gui said. "Though I haven't got over how exciting Paris was three years ago."

"Precisely," Mary said. "If—"

She broke off as Sandy Trenor came up beside him. "Thank God for friendly faces. Can I hide out with you for a bit? My mother keeps trying to put eligible girls in my way."

"My mother does the same thing with my brother," Mary said. "It can be most tiresome."

"Glad you understand, Duchess. That is, Mrs. Laclos. Laclos." Sandy nodded at Gui.

Gui, who had once avoided conventional social interactions, greeted Sandy very civilly. A short time later, he and Mary were claimed by one of her cousins. Sandy cast a glance round the ballroom, then looked from Cordelia to Harry. "Odd," Sandy said in lowered tones, as though confiding a secret. "Used to like this sort of thing well enough. One sees heaps of people one's known one's whole life. Bit monotonous, I suppose, but good for catching up with friends. And paying attention to one's relations. But now it seems devilish odd to be here without Bet. I didn't—I mean, obviously I know we can't go about together. Bet accuses me of not having a sense of how things work, but I'm not a complete idiot. It's as though I say goodbye to her and step back here, and I'm a completely different person. Only, that person seems less and less like me. I mean, obviously I'm myself, but—"

"I understand," Harry said.

Sandy tugged at his cravat. "I'm damned if I do. Or if I know what I'm going to do about it."

They'll be all right until he marries. Cordelia could hear Mélanie's words from a conversation they'd had about Sandy and Bet after they'd all dined together a month since. She touched Sandy's arm. "Perhaps the important thing is that you can be yourself with her. That's a rare thing to have with anyone, in any setting."

Sandy met her gaze for a moment, his own gaze suddenly not

as young and guileless as it often seemed. "Thank you, Lady Cordelia. That's a splendid way of putting it."

He looked so sincere. How on earth could he be the center of Elsinore League intrigues?

MÉLANIE AND MALCOLM MADE THEIR WAY TO A BAIZE-COVERED door, holding trays of empty champagne glasses for cover. They set the trays down on a table inside the door and went up the pine servants' stairs to the next floor. "Julien's here," Mélanie murmured in conversational tones.

"Well, that's interesting. Though not exactly surprising, given he knew we'd be here."

"He said he's here to help us. Though knowing Julien, I think he's more here to make mischief."

"As long as it's mischief we can turn to our advantage. I think he likes seeing you in action."

"He likes being at the center of things. Sylvie St. Ives is here too."

Malcolm paused two steps from the top. "That's a bit more worrying."

"I don't think she recognized me. Julien said he'd keep an eye on her, and I actually think he's likely to do so."

"So do I." Malcolm opened the door at the top of the stairs.

Candles burned in the wall sconces on the floor with the bedchambers. They made their way towards the room they knew was Hugh Cresswell's.

A door swung open. Malcolm grabbed Mélanie and pulled her into a shadowy doorway. They went stock still, which was much what regular footmen would do when they encountered guests in such a situation. She heard the swish of silk skirts, the patter of satin slippers, the heavier tread of a gentleman's shoes. The man gave an embarrassed laugh. The woman coughed. They hurried past.

"Easier to blend into the shadows in this garb," Malcolm murmured. "A good thing, as our usual fallback would have drawn all too much attention in this guise."

Their usual fallback was to lose themselves in an embrace as though they were bent on an amorous encounter themselves. "It's a fair question," Mélanie said. "Would two footmen sharing an embrace create more scandal than a married couple slipping upstairs for a rendezvous with each other?"

"The married couple would just cause a distraction. The footmen could get arrested."

Malcolm cast a glance up and down the passage, and they continued without incident. In Cresswell's bedchamber, Malcolm pulled a flint and a taper from his coat, lit the taper, then the Argand lamp. Mélanie glanced round the room. An oak bed, chest of drawers, dressing table, and writing desk. Blue damask hangings and upholstery. A solid, masculine look. Lady Cresswell may have chosen the furniture and embellishments, but she almost certainly had her own bedchamber. Malcolm went to the wardrobe. Mélanie went through the writing desk, the dressing table, and chest of drawers. No hidden compartments. She took things out of the chest of drawers and set them on the bed in the same order in which she'd found them, from force of habit. Though if they found the letters, it would be obvious someone had been in the room. Nothing hidden in the piles of shirts and cravats, the boxes of watch fobs and cravat pins. And then, in a plain wooden box that held handkerchiefs, a telltale crackle. She lifted out a stack of fine linen squares, worked with the Cresswell crest in the corner, and saw a bundle of papers underneath.

Odd the weight a simple stack of paper, bound up with plain buff ribbon, could hold. She'd felt it before when they'd recovered important papers. Words, as she was becoming more and more aware, could hold a great deal of power.

"I've got them," she said.

"Good work, Mel." Malcolm moved to her side.

Mélanie drew one of the letters out and unfolded it, enough to see the "My darling Anne" at the top. She counted the letters quickly. "Damnation."

"What?" Malcolm was moving the shirts and cravats back to the chest of drawers.

"There are ten letters here. Weston most specifically said there were eleven."

A further search of the room did not yield the letter. "He must have it on him," Malcolm said. "Probably as insurance. I might do the same myself. Being footmen is going to complicate getting it off him."

"What if —"

A creak sounded in the passage. Close. Not far from the door. The house was damnably quiet. They hadn't had warning and now someone was just outside the door.

Mélanie shoved the last box back in place. Malcolm grabbed her hand and they dove under the bed of one accord.

"Seems a bit cloak and dagger," a voice said. "We used to just be able to duck into the library and talk over a glass of port."

The door banged shut. "It's not the world it once was. In any number of ways." She couldn't be sure, but it sounded like Lord Beverston. "We never know who might be listening. More difficult to tell our enemies than in the old days."

"It's always difficult to tell an enemy. That's part of what makes this fun." That was the first voice. And it was a voice Mélanie knew very well. She'd heard it in the dining room less than two hours ago. It belonged to Julien St. Juste.

CHAPTER 11

"*I*t's not a game."

"No?" Julien said. "I beg to differ. But perhaps we define games differently."

"You're not taking this work seriously enough, St. Juste." That definitely was Beverston. Mélanie could picture him standing with his arms folded across his chest, impatience in his posture even in ball clothes.

"I don't believe I've actually agreed to work for you." A thud sounded. Mélanie could see Julien, perched on the dressing table, swinging one foot against its fluted leg.

"You're a fool."

"I'm a number of things," Julien said. "But I'm quite sure I'm not a fool."

"We could be the making of you."

"That assumes I'm not content with what I have now."

The other man gave a rough laugh. "You can't tell me you don't want more. Everyone does."

"Not everyone. Some seem strangely contented with their lot. Mélanie Rannoch seems oddly content. So does her husband.

Though I suppose they still want to change the world, so one can't really say they're satisfied with how things are."

"You aren't the sort to be satisfied either."

"I don't want to change the world, if that's what you mean. I quite see the problems, but as far as I'm concerned the world can take care of itself. But I do admit I tend to find the status quo boring. The question, though, is what do I want?"

"Precisely what we've been asking you." Exasperation tinged Beverston's voice. "You could have a great deal of power. You could play a deciding role in Britain."

"That sounds deadly dull. I've never been in the least interested in Britain. Or any country."

"I've seen you look at Mélanie Rannoch."

"My dear Beverston. I'm not sure what's more amusing. The idea that I could be bought with Mélanie Rannoch as an incentive or the idea that you could deliver her. If you think so, the League are guilty of grave delusions."

Mélanie felt Malcolm's taut stillness beside her.

"Everyone has a price, St. Juste."

"I doubt you could possibly determine mine. Or afford it if you could. By the way, why do you care so much about him?"

"Whom?"

"Alexander Trenor. Did you really think my sources of information were so poor?"

"There's no need for you to know. Though perhaps that's your weakness. Love of information."

"That sounds a bit more accurate than your other guesses." Julien's foot thudded against the dressing table leg. "Interesting that you care so much about young Trenor when you seem to have little enough interest in your own son."

Beverston gave a short laugh. "My son and I are hardly in agreement. Little enough reason for me to help him to any sort of preferment. Unless I fancied stabbing myself in the back."

"You're a realist, Beverston. Always liked that about you. Like to think I'd be, if I were a father, though it does seem to play havoc with the common sense of the most seemingly hardheaded people. By the way, I didn't realize Cresswell was so high in your inner circle."

"I don't believe I said he was."

"No, but you're appropriating his bedchamber as a meeting place."

"My dear St. Juste." Mélanie could almost see Beverston raise a brow. "Surely you, of all people, don't cavil at appropriating other people's private apartments for meetings. Where better to know one will be undisturbed than someone's private apartments when they are busy hosting a large entertainment?"

"A point. But obviously you aren't worried about Cresswell."

"Perhaps because I discount him." Beverston's feet thudded across the floor with a measured tread. "Our offer still stands, St. Juste. I think with time you'll see it's a far more interesting one than you're likely to receive from anyone else."

The door opened and closed. Mélanie was debating getting out and confronting Julien when the door opened again.

"I thought you'd never get rid of him." It was Sylvie St. Ives. Which was interesting, though also a complication. Mélanie felt the quickening interest radiating off Malcolm. "Does this mean you're working for the League?" Sylvie asked.

"My dear Sylvie. Do you take me for a fool?"

"You've worked for more objectionable people."

"Define objectionable." Julien paused for a moment, during which Mélanie could imagine him scanning Sylvie's features. "What do you want, *chérie*?"

"The Rannochs are looking for something."

"It wouldn't surprise me. They're usually involved in some intrigue or other. But they aren't here tonight."

"No, but Harry and Cordelia Davenport are. I imagine Malcolm and Mélanie sent them."

"Why don't you ask them?"

"Don't play games, Julien. The Rannochs are looking for letters that could be damaging to a certain member of the government."

"That could be any one of a dozen political scandals."

"To Lord Weston."

"Well, that's interesting. And Fouché wants these letters too?"

"I didn't say I was working for Fouché."

"Now you have me intrigued."

"You, of all people, know about serving different masters."

"So I do. At the moment I'm attempting to serve no one."

"You'll get bored without an assignment."

"We're talking about Weston."

"You can't tell me you feel any particular loyalty to Lord Weston."

"You could say I'm inclined to support anyone the League are targeting, on general principles."

"Since when you do have principles of any sort?"

"I don't like being used. I don't like my talents being taken advantage of."

"And you're helping the Rannochs."

"My dear Sylvie. What on earth gave you that idea?"

"I know you, Julien."

"I don't know that anyone knows me. You may have greater insights than some, I confess."

"Mélanie Rannoch is your weakness."

"My dear Sylvie. That sounds like something out of a play."

"I wouldn't have thought it at first, given her own past, but I think she means to you what Oliver does to me. A promise of a life we never had. That we know we wouldn't be suited for. But we can't quite stop imagining what it might have been like. I didn't realize you had those thoughts until recently."

"I didn't realize it at all. Do go on. This is most intriguing. Even if it's entirely without basis in reality."

Beside Mélanie, Malcolm remained completely still. She could feel him taking the information in like a professional. She couldn't have said whether or how he was evaluating it on any other level. "I don't think you've ever forgiven me for telling Carfax about Mélanie," Sylvie said.

"That was stupid. I was stupid for giving you information that let you piece together the truth."

"Even you are prone to careless confidences."

"So it would seem." Julien's voice had taken on a harder edge.

"You're a bit sympathetic to Malcolm Rannoch as well."

"My dear girl. Whatever experiments I may indulge in, I assure you I have no interest in Malcolm Rannoch."

"I didn't mean that sort of interest. You like him."

"I don't 'like' anyone."

"Call it what you will. Are you working with Carfax?"

"Am I what?" Julien demanded.

"Don't deny you've talked to him."

"It's difficult to entirely avoid talking to him."

"You haven't entirely broken ties with him."

"Despite our successes a year ago, you can't be so naïve as to think either of us will ever entirely break ties with him. And you can't deny that he's useful."

"I can't believe you could forget what he's done to us."

"My dear Sylvie." Julien's voice was suddenly and unexpectedly hard. "I haven't forgot anything."

"Well, then. He'll always be a threat."

"And better to know what he's doing."

"Is that it? Or are you afraid of what would happen if Carfax was suddenly out of the way?"

"That would be interesting. But seems so unlikely that I scarcely waste time on it."

"You may ignore it, but I rather think that's because it terrifies you."

"And if you're suggesting we get rid of him, need I remind you that he still has some information he can use to control us?"

"As if I could forget."

A faint stir indicated Julien had got to his feet. "You must want to get back to the ballroom if you think something's afoot there. I'll be the gentleman and let you leave first. If anyone notices, there'll be a quite obvious explanation for our seeking refuge in a bedchamber."

Sylvie gave a dry laugh. "There was a time when that wouldn't have been so funny about us."

"There was a time when we were a lot of things."

The door clicked open and shut.

"YOU CAN COME OUT, MÉLANIE. RANNOCH. SORRY ABOUT SYLVIE. She can be hard to get rid of." Julien's face came into view beneath the velvet counterpane on Cresswell's bed. He held out his hand to help Mélanie get to her feet.

"Did you know we were here when you brought Beverston in?" she asked.

"I did not bring Beverston in. I was surprised and not happy when he insisted on talking here. Because having seen you both leave the ballroom—with your usual discretion—I suspected you were here. But I also knew if I made too much of a fuss I'd rouse his suspicions. Did you find the papers?"

"One's missing."

"Damnation."

"What do you know about the letters?" Malcolm asked, springing to his feet beside Mélanie.

"What I learned from your sister."

"And you want to help Weston?"

"I want to check the League. As I told you yesterday. As you heard me tell Sylvie just now."

Malcolm held Julien with a gaze like the flat of a sword blade. "Why do you think the League are interested in Sandy Trenor?"

"I'm as mystified as you are."

"What about Sylvie?" Mélanie asked.

Julien frowned. "I don't know whom she's working for. Or why the interest in Weston and young Trenor. Which seems somewhat out of proportion to the degree of power Weston wields or the talents of the agreeable Mr. Trenor." Julien twitched a shirt cuff straight. "Sorry you overheard her overdramatic speculation."

"Nothing I didn't already suspect myself," Malcolm said.

Julien shot a look at him. "More fool you, then."

"I may well be fortune's fool, but I think I have as much insight as Sylvie St. Ives when it comes to your feelings towards Mélanie. When it comes to me, you scarcely know me."

"Quite so." Julien smoothed the other shirt cuff. "It seems we're in agreement about one thing, at least. Hadn't we best think about how we're going to get the missing letter back?"

"I don't think there's any 'we' about it, Julien," Mélanie said.

"Oh, well, if you don't want my help—"

"Actually we could probably use it," Malcolm said.

"Darling," Mélanie said.

"Always knew you were a pragmatist, Rannoch," Julien said.

"Between being in disguise and being objects of suspicion if we leave off our disguise, we're at a disadvantage," Malcolm said.

"Oh, all right," Mélanie conceded. "I suppose it wouldn't come amiss. But you're running backup on this mission, Julien."

"I'm perfectly capable of running backup. It's a positive relief at times."

"Ha. We'd better find Harry and Cordy."

MALCOLM FOUND HARRY ON THE EDGE OF THE DANCE FLOOR. Harry snagged a glass of champagne from the tray Malcolm had retrieved when he came back downstairs. "Complications?"

"Cresswell seems to have one of the letters on him. We're

going to need both of you." Malcolm scanned the ballroom for Cordelia.

"She's dancing with Gui." Harry jerked his head towards the country dance that was in progress. Cordelia, the cherry ribbons on her gown swirling round her, twirled beneath Gui Laclos's arm. The lack of concern in Harry's voice said wonders about where he and his wife had arrived.

Harry caught Cordelia's eye and raised his glass in what might have been an inconsequential gesture. Cordy inclined her head in a way that might have been equally inconsequential to one not trained to notice such things. When the dance came to an end, she moved to Harry's and Malcolm's side. St. Juste joined them as well.

"Am I heartless to confess I'm glad the two of you didn't get to have all the fun?" Cordelia said, when Malcolm explained the situation.

"Spoken like a true agent, Lady Cordelia," St. Juste murmured. "Which could also mean heartless."

Cordelia spared him a smile. "Can I take it while dancing with Cresswell?" she asked.

"That was my first thought," Malcolm said. "But we don't know where he has it. It may not be conveniently tucked into his coat. We're going to need to get him alone and disable him. And he's not going to leave the room with a hired footman, and he'll likely be on his guard with you and Harry. We need reinforcements."

A slow smile crossed Cordelia's face. "What a lucky thing we're all friends. And she is a spymaster's daughter, after all."

CHAPTER 12

Cordelia and Mary Laclos approached Hugh Cresswell where he stood talking with the Duke of Wellington and Lord Sidmouth. Mary's reticule slipped from her fingers just as they passed the men and tumbled to the polished floorboards right by Cresswell's feet. "Permit me, Duchess. Mrs. Laclos, that is." He bent to retrieve the reticule and handed it back to her.

"Thank you. So silly of me," said Mary, who never used words like 'silly,' especially about herself. She leaned forwards to take the reticule, then stumbled and fell against Cresswell. "Oh, dear."

"Mary," Cordelia reached for her friend.

"The silliest thing." Mary clung to Cresswell. "But I'm afraid I feel quite light-headed."

"It's no wonder, you've just had a baby," Cordelia said.

"Perhaps you could sit on one of the sofas?" Cresswell suggested.

"Oh, no, Gui will fuss and I'll have all the dowagers gossip about me. If you could just help me into one of the anterooms. I believe that door leads to one."

"I'll bring your reticule." Cordelia took the reticule from Cresswell, then moved ahead and opened the anteroom door. Cresswell helped Mary into the room. Mary collapsed on a sofa not far from the door. "Oh, dear, I've turned into such a poor creature. Perhaps you could pour me a glass of that sherry?"

Cresswell moved to a table with decanters that stood before a window veiled in green velvet. As he turned to pick up the decanter, Malcolm emerged from behind the curtains and hit him over the head with the flat of his hand. Cresswell crumpled to the ground, spilling the contents of the decanter over himself.

"Neatly done." Mélanie emerged from another set of curtains.

"Not so neatly." Malcolm flexed his fingers. "I used to be able to do that without feeling as though I'd broken every bone in my hand. And I was trying to get him before he picked up the decanter."

"The spilled sherry will explain why he's lying on the floor if anyone happens upon him." Mélanie was already on her knees beside Cresswell, pushing back his coat.

"Good heavens, Malcolm," Mary said from the sofa. She hadn't, Cordelia realized, seen Malcolm in action as much as Cordelia had herself. "Where did you learn to do that?"

"O'Roarke taught me. When I was about twelve. At the time, I took it for granted that he knew how to do such things." Malcolm knelt opposite Mélanie. "Anything, Mel?"

"Not yet." Mélanie unbuttoned Cresswell's waistcoat.

Cordelia knelt beside her. "It's a good thing we didn't try to pick his pockets on the dance floor." She tugged Cresswell's shirt free from his breeches and reached under the linen. Something crackled beneath her fingers. She drew out a single sheet of paper, covered with crossed lines. She handed it to Mélanie.

"It's Weston's hand," Mélanie said with a sigh of relief. "The inscription and signature are both there. We have it. The whole letter." She sat back on her heels.

"What an adventure," Mary said. "I feel like a girl again instead of a twice-married mother of four. Not that I did this sort of thing when I was a girl. I suppose it's the sort of thing you do all the time?"

"Hardly," Malcolm said.

Mélanie checked Cresswell's pulse. "Regular. He should come to shortly. Best make ourselves scarce."

Malcolm pushed himself to his feet and reached out a hand to Mélanie and Cordelia. As he helped them to their feet, three quick raps sounded on the connecting door from the salon. Harry's signal. Cordelia ran to open the door to let him in.

Harry cast a quick glance at Cresswell. "Got the letter?"

"All accounted for," Mélanie said.

"That's good. We've had some complications. Apparently they've tumbled to there being interlopers among the footmen. I overheard the butler talking to one of the regular footmen."

Mélanie exchanged a look with Malcolm. "Fortunately, we're prepared," Mélanie said. She ducked down and retrieved a canvas bag she'd stashed beneath the sofa earlier in the evening. "Give us two minutes and we can turn back into ourselves."

"But won't they know why you're here?" Mary asked.

"Cresswell's the one who would have been likeliest to put it together, and he's out of commission." Malcolm shrugged out of his footman's coat. "Beverston or someone else in the League might be on the look-out, but now we have the letters they can't do much. Except try to do to us what we did to Cresswell, I suppose, but we're prepared and we have backup."

Cordelia and Mary shielded Mélanie while she pulled off her heavy footman's coat, unbuttoned the stiff waistcoat, unwound the lace-edged cravat. She had the silver silk slip of her gown on under her shirt, rolled up to help pad her figure. Clever, Cordelia thought. Mélanie removed her knee breeches beneath the slip. Cordelia helped her into her smoke grey crêpe robe. Mélanie did up the pearl clasps and replaced her heavy white stockings and silver-buckled shoes with the sheer silk stockings worked with clocks and satin-ribboned slippers Mary pulled from the canvas bag. Mélanie pulled off her wig and pushed her fingers into her hair to loosen it about her face, added her diamond earrings and wedding ring (she'd had her necklace on beneath her shirt). A quick glance in the mirror and she added rouge and eye blacking, then pulled on her gloves and picked up her reticule and shawl.

"I don't think that even took two minutes," Mary said. "It takes me half an hour to dress on a good day."

"And the effect is much more impressive." Mélanie smoothed her gloves and draped her shawl over her arms. "But this should pass muster late in the evening when the candles are beginning to gutter."

"And fortunately no one expects sartorial brilliance from me." Malcolm was finishing tying his cravat. He was attired in black trousers and coat and a gray silk waistcoat. Harry dusted stray traces of wig powder from his shoulders with professional skill.

They stuffed their footmen's clothes and wigs into the canvas bag and stashed it under the sofa, and cast one more glance at Cresswell, who was still unconscious though breathing regularly.

"Surely when he comes to he'll realize what's happened," Mary said.

"Yes, but we'll be gone with the letters." Malcolm tucked a chintz sofa cushion beneath Cresswell's head. "He won't be able to do anything about it. And he won't be sure how witting a role you played."

"Oh, I'm not worried about that." Mary's ruby bracelet flashed in the candlelight as she waved a white-gloved hand. "Actually, I should quite like staring him down and daring him to accuse me."

Cordelia smoothed a smudge off Mélanie's face. "Rather convenient not to need to care about our position in society. It takes away so many problems."

❧

THEY RETURNED TO THE BALLROOM THROUGH THE SALON.

Malcolm went out first with Cordelia and Mary on each arm. He didn't look over his shoulder, but he heard the swish of Mélanie's skirt as she and Harry followed. Julien exchanged a look with Mélanie and then with Malcolm from across the room and melted into the shadows. Malcolm couldn't see Sylvie in the immediate vicinity.

Gui came up beside them. "Missed all the fun," he murmured.

"Next time." Mary tucked her arm through her husband's own. "I should dearly love to stay to see how this plays out, but I suppose we should be sensible and go home."

Malcolm took her hand. "Thank you, Mary."

Mary pressed his hand. "And perhaps this doesn't need saying, but I won't say a word to Father. Whatever you're doing, I don't see that he needs to know anything about it."

"Thank you, Mary," Malcolm said again, in more fervent tones.

"Schoolroom solidarity has to mean something."

"Mélanie. I no idea you were here." Emily Cowper swept up to them in a stir of jade satin and emeralds. "What a wretch you are not to tell me when you finally emerge in society. It's good to see you too, Malcolm." She leaned forwards to accept Malcolm's kiss on her cheek.

"We only looked in very briefly, Emily," Mélanie said. "Jessica was fretful, so I wasn't sure we'd make it at all."

"Malcolm—" Mary drew Malcolm a little aside as Harry, Mélanie, and Gui exchanged the necessary pleasantries with Emily. "I heard you called on Father recently."

"I had some business to discuss with him."

Mary scanned his face. "Not that I can't understand someone falling out with my father, but I'm sorry you aren't the friends you once were. I never thought I'd say this about him, but I think he could use a friend now." She fingered the ebony sticks of her fan. "I count myself a woman of the world, but I never expected coldness between my parents."

Malcolm studied his childhood friend. "It's hard to know what goes on inside a marriage, Mary. Sometimes one can misjudge from the outside."

"As I know better than any. Still—they're perfectly polite. They appear together in society as much as ever. They seem to spend as much time together. But something isn't the same." She frowned. "It's odd. Until I married Gui, I'm not sure I'd have noticed the difference. Just as I'm not sure I'd have noticed whatever seems to be amiss between Bel and Oliver, though they seem to be on a bit better terms these days. I'm glad David's out of it." She looked at Malcolm, brows raised. "Surprised? I never was quite as heartless as everyone seems to think. And I'm the last to worry about society's opinion now. At first I thought Mama and Father had quarreled over David, and I thought the better of Mama for standing up to Father, but I don't think that's it. More's the pity, if they had to quarrel about something. I would think one of them had a lover, except with them, it's patently absurd."

Malcolm touched her arm. "They have a lot of history to build on, Mary. That will help them sort it out."

Her gaze moved across his face. "So confident they will sort it out? I'm not Lucinda, Malcolm. You don't have to sugarcoat things for me."

"I'd never think I could, Mary. I know your parents. I know what they mean to each other."

"I thought I did." Mary hesitated a moment, then shook her head. "I shouldn't keep you longer, and we need to get home to the baby." She gathered the folds of her shawl up about her shoulders. "We'll see you at the wedding."

"Thank you for coming. It means a lot to Raoul and Laura, and to Mélanie and me as well."

"My dear Malcolm. Laura's my stepdaughter-in-law, after all."

And Mary's late husband had been Laura's lover, though Malcolm profoundly hoped Mary never learned that. "Your parents will be there as well."

"Yes, that surprised me. Perhaps a sign that Father is mellowing a bit. Or is he there to work?"

"I don't think so."

"If I were a romantic I'd hope the wedding stirs memories in my parents." Mary smiled at her husband. "But of course I'm a hardhearted realist, as you well know."

"I won't let your secret out."

Mary pressed his arm. "Thank you for the adventure, Malcolm."

"RANNOCH. DIDN'T KNOW YOU WERE HERE."

"Sandy." Malcolm smiled at his young friend. He, Mélanie, Cordelia, and Harry had just moved, without enough haste to draw attention, round the edge of the ballroom and through the archway, into the first-floor hall. "We just popped in briefly. You've caught us on our way out. Jessica was fretful, and Mel has a dreadful headache."

Mélanie gave a grimace that could well betoken as much, though Malcolm knew she would tease him about making her seem sadly insipid afterwards.

"This won't take long, but I need to talk to you." Sandy's voice was low and urgent. "I've just remembered something."

"We'll order the carriage," Harry said. "Always takes a devilish long time."

"I think there's an antechamber through that door," Sandy said, indicating the room they had recently vacated.

"No, let's go downstairs." Malcolm put a hand on Sandy's shoulder. They went down the staircase, only having to stop to exchange nods twice and answer exclamations of surprise at their presence three times. Mélanie, Cordelia, and Harry went to retrieve wraps and order the carriage. Malcolm steered Sandy into Cresswell's study. Which, as things had gone, they hadn't had to search earlier.

"I was talking to Mama about Aunt Anne and Weston," Sandy said in swift, urgent tones. "You were right. They were in love. Mama admitted Aunt Anne thought of herself as betrothed to Weston. The thing is, though, I didn't have the sense Mama was very fond of Weston. She said Aunt Anne had a lucky escape. I asked her what she meant because he seems so ordinary. Well, he did until you started asking questions about him, but I didn't say that part. Mama said Weston was involved in things that were dangerous. That she'd never have credited it but for things Aunt Anne told her when she— Aunt Anne—and Weston were unofficially betrothed. Of course I asked her what on earth she was talking about, and Mama said it had actually proved to be an unexpected adventure."

Malcolm clapped him on the shoulder. "Thank you, Sandy."

"Is it important?" Sandy scanned his face.

"It may be. I'm not quite sure how yet." He hesitated a moment. "Are your parents particular friends of the Cresswells?"

"Oh, yes, have been for years. They dined with the Cresswells just a fortnight ago. Mama seemed quite animated afterwards. I thought at the time it was good for her to get out. Does Cresswell have something to do with Weston's letters? "

"He seems to have been the one who took them. We got them back tonight."

Sandy let out a whistle. "I still can't make sense of how all these people who seemed stodgy when I was in the nursery have been up to all manner of skullduggery." He drew a breath, as though on the verge of saying more, but when he finally spoke Malcolm had the sense it wasn't what he had almost said. "I won't mention anything to Mama."

Malcolm swallowed. Like Mary, Sandy grasped the essentials, though he understood less of the larger picture.

They went out into the passage. Footsteps sounded on the

stairs. Malcolm looked up to see Cresswell staring down at him. "My compliments, Rannoch."

"I don't deserve them."

"This is only a skirmish."

Cresswell held Malcolm's gaze for a long moment. Then, as two ladies descended the stairs behind him, he turned round with the smiling mask of a convivial host.

"What was that about?" Sandy demanded as he Malcolm moved into the hall.

"A minor conflict."

"And you bested him?"

"I wouldn't say that. We may have come out ahead for the moment."

CHAPTER 13

"I feel quite useless," Raoul said. "And distinctly proud."

Malcolm grinned at his father. "It was a simple mission."

"A simple mission with complications. Which you handled superbly."

They were gathered in the Berkeley Square library over coffee and whisky, those who had gone to the Cresswell ball and those who had remained behind. Malcolm wasn't sure which group had found the evening more challenging.

"You think Sandy's mother leaked the Craanford information?" Cordelia said with the disbelief of one who had known Lady Marchmain since childhood. Of course, Malcolm had known Raoul and Archie since childhood. It all depended on one's perspective.

"I think it's possible," Malcolm said. "The likeliest explanation we've hit upon so far."

"So Lady Darlington didn't betray Weston," Mélanie said.

"I suspect not. And if I'm right, Lady Marchmain may have told Cresswell about the letters."

"Which raises the question of whether Lady Marchmain is working with the League." Frances turned to Archie.

"I never heard anything to suggest it," Archie said. "Nor to suggest she's Cresswell's mistress. But of course one—or both—is quite possible."

"It's a good theory," Raoul said. "Lady Marchmain—Helen Angelsley, as she was then—would have been almost the last person we'd have suspected at the time of the Craanford leak. It certainly explains why we could never discover the source of the leak at the time. Not that I couldn't have missed something, but I investigated the obvious suspects enough that I always thought perhaps it was someone unlikely. In which case we have the question of whom she was giving the information to. Not Cresswell, as far as I know. I don't know the family well, but I don't think they were players in Irish or British politics."

"Alistair Rannoch?" Cordelia asked. "Though I suppose there's nothing to suggest he had any connection to the Trenor family or to Helen Angelsley going so far back."

"Lady Marchmain's elder son ended up working for the League," Laura pointed out.

"So he did." Raoul took a sip of whisky. "And we've thought it was simply for the money, that he didn't know what he was involved in. This may make that question worth a second look. And the League want to secure her younger son's preferment."

Cordelia set down her glass. "Are you saying you suspect Sandy?"

"I see no reason to. He'd hardly have told Malcolm the story in that case. Unless the whole is a very elaborate set up. But the Trenor family seem to have more to do with the League than we at first thought."

"At least Lord Weston is free from pressure," Frances said. "And there's nothing to stop him from pursuing a relationship with Anne Darlington now."

"Nothing except his own qualms." Raoul reached for Laura's hand. "I hope he can overcome them."

WESTON GLANCED ROUND THE COFFEEHOUSE IN PICCADILLY, crowded with a midmorning jumble of journalists, law clerks, tradesmen, and a smattering of well-dressed gentlemen. "A surprising choice for a meeting," he said as he pulled out a chair at the table Raoul had chosen at the back.

Raoul took a sip of coffee. "I've always conducted some of my most sensitive meetings in coffeehouses. Sometimes it's easiest to exchange information in public. Nothing like crowd noise for cover. And we don't have to worry about the League anymore." He drew the letters out from inside his coat and placed them on the table.

Weston stared down at the packet of papers as though they might be a mirage. "I trusted you. I know how good you are at what you do. But I don't think I quite believed—I can't thank you enough."

Raoul signaled to a waiter to bring Weston coffee. "It was Malcolm and Mélanie who got them back. I think they relished the adventure, as well as being able to outwit the Elsinore League."

"And you still don't know why they wanted Alexander Trenor given the junior secretaryship?"

"No." Raoul hesitated a moment, but Weston deserved to know and he might have valuable intelligence. "Did Lady Darlington—Miss Somercote—confide a great deal in her cousin Helen?"

"Helen Marchmain? Trenor's mother?" Weston's fingers tightened on the letters. "Sure you don't think—"

"According to something Sandy Trenor told Malcolm last night, Lady Marchmain was aware of your activities in Ireland and wasn't happy about them."

"And that makes you think—"

"The League are scheming to elevate her son. The League found out about the letters. If Lady Marchmain knew about the letters, it seems plausible she told the League, and if she's connected to them in some capacity that might explain their interest in Sandy Trenor."

Weston's brows drew together. Duplicity, particularly in a woman, shocked him, but he wasn't a slow man. "Anne and Helen have always been close. I know Anne confided in Helen about our attachment. It wouldn't be surprising if she told her about my activities. For God's sake, they were cousins. Childhood friends. Anne would have trusted her."

"Yes. Breaches of intelligence usually come from someone that someone else trusted."

"And you exploit those breaches."

Raoul met his former comrade's gaze. "Yes, I have. I do. Including at times with those closest to me. No one could blame Lady Darlington for confiding in her friend, but someone in search of intelligence, who had the present Lady Marchmain's confidence, might have been quick to exploit that trust."

Weston went silent as a waiter put a cup of coffee in front of him. He murmured his thanks, took a sip of coffee, and studied Raoul for a long moment. "Craanford. You never learned who was behind it. I know you wondered about me."

"I wondered about everyone."

"And you think Helen—"

"I think it's the most plausible explanation we've hit on yet. It doesn't prove anything."

Weston lifted his cup and blew on the steam. "So this isn't over."

"Nothing's over with the Elsinore League."

"Or with whatever they're trying to accomplish with Sandy Trenor."

"Perhaps not. But I don't think they'll try to move against you again. You have the letters. You can burn them, unless you can't bear to part with them."

"Shouldn't a spymaster scoff at any such romantic impulse?"

"Perhaps spymasters particularly understand the challenge of romantic impulses. And the need to have the courage to pursue them." Raoul reached for his own coffee. "Of course, if you really wanted to pursue such an impulse, you could consider a future with Lady Darlington."

Weston looked down at the letters and drew a breath.

Raoul took a sip of coffee. Strong, slightly bitter, bracing, a constant in his life from Ireland to Paris to Spain to Britain. "Laura and I would be delighted to have you at the wedding. But I understand if you think it prudent not to advertise any connection between us."

Weston lifted his coffee to Raoul's in a silent toast and gave a sudden grin. "I'll be damned if I'll let prudence make me turn my back on a friend. I'd be honored, O'Roarke."

CHAPTER 14

"*N*ervous?" Malcolm asked.

Raoul adjusted a fold of his cravat in the looking glass. "Why would I be nervous? It's not as though it changes anything for Laura and me. We've been living as though we were married at least since Italy."

Malcolm had been nervous on his own wedding day, but close as he and Raoul now were, that hardly seemed an occasion to bring up. He'd invited Raoul to his own wedding to Mel almost six years ago. Raoul had declined, saying business called him out of Lisbon. Malcolm had been sorry at the time, but in retrospect he could certainly understand why. "There's something about the officialness of it. Or perhaps of being in front of so many of one's friends and family."

"Not to mention former enemies and uncertain allies." Raoul pulled a pearl pin from the cravat and adjusted a fold. "I'm not nervous. I'm rather stunned this is happening at all." He twitched a crease smooth in the linen. "At the risk of giving way to sentiment, it's somewhat overwhelming to be happier than one ever expected to be."

"You're going to ruin that cravat if you fuss with it any more."

Malcolm took the pin from Raoul and arranged it in the snowy folds. "For as long as I can remember, you could tie a cravat effortlessly. You taught me."

"The linen's a bit overstarched."

"Seems perfectly all right to me." Malcolm made a last adjustment to the neckcloth. "I can understand it being overwhelming. You never thought you had the right to be happy."

"My dear Malcolm." Raoul's gaze was on the looking glass. "I've hardly been suffering. And I've known a great deal of happiness. More, one could argue, than I deserve."

"My point precisely." Malcolm brushed a speck of lint from the glossy blue superfine of his father's coat. "And it's folly to talk about deserving."

"All right, yes." Raoul frowned into the glass. "I have good fortune I never thought to have, and this day somehow cements it all. These past months we've been so focused on getting to it, I think a part of me couldn't quite believe it would really happen. And it reminds me of how very much I have to lose."

"The Elsinore League aren't going to stop you from marrying Laura."

"Not that, my good idiot. I'm afraid of bungling it myself. As I have a history of doing."

Malcolm looked at his father. Immaculately arrayed, but somehow he seemed as young as Colin for a moment. Though one had a lot more regrets at one-and-fifty than at almost six. "You learn from your mistakes, O'Roarke. And there's a lot you haven't bungled. Me, for instance."

Raoul turned from the mirror and put a hand on Malcolm's shoulder. "Have I told you how proud I am of you, Malcolm?"

Malcolm grinned. "I think the subject's come up."

～

"You look pretty, Mummy."

Laura smiled at her daughter, who was perched on the edge of the bed between Colin and Livia Davenport. "I look like I'm about to have a baby, which is certainly the case. Thank goodness for the current fashions. I can't imagine doing this in a hoop skirt."

"I think you look pretty with the baby in your tummy," Emily said.

"Thank you, sweetheart."

"So do I," Colin said. "Mummy was pretty when she was going to have Jessica."

"Throw flowers?" Jessica tugged at Mélanie's sapphire silk skirt.

"Soon." Mélanie bent down to twitch Jessica's blue satin sash smooth, then did the same for Drusilla. Colin, Emily, and Livia were sitting very still in their wedding finery. Keeping them immaculate for the wedding wouldn't be a problem. The little girls were a different story. Not that it really mattered. Laura wouldn't mind and Raoul certainly wouldn't. It was hardly, as Laura was quick to point out, a society wedding. Still, for one who had grown up in the theatre, a smooth production could not but be an aim.

Cordelia slipped into the room. "Most of the guests are here. Valentin and Michael are passing round champagne and everyone's happy." She paused for a moment, taking in Laura in her gown of pale blue tulle, with the same sapphire blue ribbon as the girls. "Oh, you do look lovely, Laura. I must say the glow of pregnancy is quite an asset to a bride. Pity more aren't able to take advantage of it."

Laura laughed. But there was a glow in her eyes that had nothing to do with pregnancy and everything to do with sheer happiness.

They moved into the passage to go down to the drawing room where the guests were gathered. Colin caught Jessica by the hand and Livia, Drusilla. The children clustered round Laura. "It's wonderful," Cordelia murmured to Mélanie, as they left the room.

"To be so happy on one's wedding day. And so sure. I was rather terrified. About what I'd got myself into."

"So was I." Mélanie remembered that December morning in Lisbon. The unreality of it. And the shocking truth of hearing Malcolm reciting his wedding vows. "But it worked out rather well for both of us."

～

SHE LOOKED LOVELY. ODD, HE HADN'T EXPECTED THAT. OR, RATHER, hadn't been focused on it. She was always beautiful. He was aware of that, just as he was aware of her brilliance, and her warmth, and all the other things that made her Laura. But he hadn't somehow been prepared for this woman he knew so well to take his breath away.

She looked into his eyes and smiled as though she too was aware of the unreality of the situation.

He murmured his vows. Laura murmured hers with a faint lift of her brow at "obey." Malcolm put the ring in his hand. He slid it onto Laura's finger, as he had once slid his signet ring on her finger, at a time when marriage had seemed an impossibility.

And it was done. They were married. He tightened his grip on Laura's hand and reached out to pull Emily to them. Not the conventional conclusion to a wedding, but then their guests knew they weren't conventional.

～

AMAZING HOW DIFFERENT THE SAME WORDS COULD SOUND. SHE'D repeated these vows with Jack. She still didn't agree with all the words, but the underlying promises she and Raoul were making rang through her. Her father had walked her down the aisle then as well. She'd been grateful for his support but conscious that she'd disappointed him. Odd, from the outside you'd think it was this wedding, eight months pregnant, to a divorced man, that would concern a father, but he was misty-eyed with genuine parental happiness. Her stepmother, Sarah, had been at her first wedding as well. They were much better friends now, and her eldest half-sister, who had sat on Sarah's lap then, was now one of her young attendants.

The other guests were all new. A different country, a different group of people, a new family she'd created while forging stronger ties with her original family. A daughter she hadn't even dreamed of then, smiling at the edge of her skirts and holding the bridal bouquet with grown-up concentration.

A different man, a man she knew as she'd never known Jack, a man she loved with an intensity she wouldn't have thought possible, that she couldn't begin to put into words, that frightened her sometimes in ways she wouldn't admit to anyone, because one couldn't love this strongly without appalling risk.

He slid the ring onto her finger. She smiled up into his eyes. He drew Emily to them. They stood for a moment, Emily and the unborn baby between them. They'd been a family for a long time. But now the world knew they were one.

CHAPTER 15

*A*melia Carfax tucked a handkerchief into her reticule. "I always cry at weddings. Mary accuses me of dreadful sentimentality."

"I confess I shed a tear or two at this one myself," Frances said. "And normally I make it a point never to cry in public."

Amelia snapped the reticule closed. "It's particularly gratifying given the challenges they've faced."

"And because they genuinely care for each other."

"Yes, it appears they do." Amelia regarded the couple for a moment across the Berkeley Square drawing room. Raoul had his arm round Laura, and Emily on his shoulders. "That's not necessarily a guarantee of anything. But I think when a man lives a life like Mr. O'Roarke, it's as well his wife is a bit older and clear-eyed going into the marriage."

Frances took a sip of champagne, searching for the right words. She and Amelia had never been confidantes. But they were at least friends, and Amelia probably had few, if any, friends who knew the source of the tension in her marriage. "I always thought you understood the challenges of being married to Hubert. Though I imagine the challenges were considerable."

"Yes, on both counts. It helps not to have illusions. I imagine Laura Tarrington—Laura O'Roarke—doesn't. I never have."

"That doesn't necessarily make certain truths easy to hear."

"No, it doesn't. Though nothing I've heard recently is anything I didn't know, or at least suspect, long since." She met Frances's gaze for a moment. Amelia was a woman who kept appearances in place the same way she made sure her rouge was perfectly blended, her bonnet precisely tied, her gloves without a crease. In her own way, she was every bit as good at playing a role as her husband, Frances realized. And yet now the customary veil was gone. Frances wondered if there were moments when spies looked at fellow spies as directly. "Your sister was a complicated woman, Fanny. I felt sorry for her. I admired her at times. I confess at other times she frustrated me, mostly when Malcolm was staying with us and it was so clear to me he wanted more from her." She hesitated a moment. Her gaze went from Mélanie, who was carrying Jessica and Drusilla in each arm, heedless of the creases in her sapphire silk gown, to Laura and Raoul, who were now kneeling to look at a book with Emily and Colin, and then to her own daughter Mary, who had her baby in her arms. "Not that I'm immune to questioning my own choices."

"I've certainly questioned mine." Frances looked at Archie and Chloe, who each had one of the babies. Parenthood had evolved for her. It had been different (and far more agreeable) with Chloe than with her first-born, Cedric, but it was a whole new experience this time. Partly because it was twins, but mostly because of Archie.

"I'm impressed," Amelia said. "With your ability to question. And you're fortunate to have the chance to do certain things again. Of course, agreeable as the world the Rannochs have created may be, it's not the world we live in. In any case, though I may have occasionally blamed Arabella when it came to Malcolm, I don't blame her for the events of which there is no sense pretending we have not all become recently apprised." She smoothed a crease from her glove. "In fact, I was quite certain of those events at the time they occurred. Which should make learning the truth easier. Six months ago I'd have said I was at peace with it. But somehow actually hearing it is different."

"There's a difference between suspicions and reality," Frances said. "One has no 'perhaps' to hide behind."

"Yes." Amelia cast a brief look at her husband. He was talking to Frances's daughter Aline and Allie's husband Geoffrey Blackwell, a doctor who would be called to deliver Laura's baby before too much longer. Carfax's back to was them, but Frances sensed he was acutely aware of Amelia and probably guessed the topic of their conversation. "Six months ago I'd have said I saw Hubert clearly. That I loved him with clear-eyed wisdom. Now I think I was living with illusions for the almost four decades of my marriage."

Sympathy was not a feeling Frances was inclined to associate with Amelia Carfax, but now she reached out without thinking and put a hand on the other woman's arm. "I'd never have called you blind, observing you with Hubert. But I think perhaps there are things we all have to choose not to dwell on to make relationships work."

"Spoken as a new bride?" Amelia lifted a brow.

"Spoken as a woman with considerable experience of relationships—most of which I would call unsuccessful—who is endeavoring to make this one work."

"You look happy, Fanny. In a way I've never seen you."

"I am happy." It was not something Frances would have admitted to a year and a half, even a year, ago.

"As I said, marrying later in life seems to have much to recommend it." Amelia's gaze drifted over the company. "I didn't realize Sandy Trenor was here."

"He and Malcolm and Mélanie have become quite close."

"Who's that young woman with him?"

"Miss Elizabeth Simcox. A friend of Malcolm and Mélanie's as well."

"I don't know the name." Amelia studied Bet. In a demure gown of cherry-sprigged muslin, her hair in ringlets and a simple knot, her face bare of rouge (or very nearly so) she looked like any other young woman in Mayfair who was present. "Good heavens, is that the girl—"

"Sandy's very fond of her as well," Frances said. Thank God for a position that made navigating the shoals of society relatively easy for her daughters. It made life so much simpler. A secure place in society made it so much easier to be a revolutionary.

"Malcolm's never given much heed to the forms. But I thought Mélanie was a bit more careful, at least for his sake. Not to mention her children's."

"I think Italy changed a lot for both of them. And as to the children, I think she wants them to grow up knowing the people she cares about."

"Sandy does appear happy." Amelia watched him for a moment, standing very correctly not too close to Bet, but with his head angled towards hers. "But I do hope he has a care for his parents' sake. It can't but be a challenging time for the family. Especially as Matt's exile leaves Sandy as the potential heir."

"He can't inherit the title," Frances said. "But even if he could, why should it matter?" She stared at Amelia, because when a younger son's becoming the heir was an issue, it usually meant one thing. "Goodness, I never realized—"

"It's only inference." Amelia watched her for a moment. "But somehow I thought you'd know. Though perhaps it makes sense that he'd have been at pains to keep it from you."

"Who?" Frances stared at Amelia. Fragments of conversation from the night Malcolm and Mélanie had recovered Lord Weston's letters echoed in her head. Helen Marchmain had probably betrayed the United Irishmen to someone. And perhaps told the League about Weston's role in the Irish uprising and told Hugh

Cresswell about the letters. "Amelia, are you suggesting Alistair was Sandy Trenor's father?"

"Dear God." Amelia put a hand to her head. "It's not like me to gossip this way. I haven't been myself. I suppose one could say Malcolm should know. Given how close they've become, I thought perhaps he did. Though it's not as if it makes them brothers." She cast a quick glance at Raoul. "So many things seem to be an open secret these days. I'm talking out of turn."

"On the contrary," Frances said. "I'm very glad I know. In fact, this could be vital."

"Vital to what?" Amelia asked.

"Understanding the past."

"It's good to see you both here." Malcolm stopped beside Sandy and Bet.

"It's so lovely." For once Bet didn't hang back and leave it to Sandy to speak first. "They look so happy. It obviously means so much to them."

"Yes." Sandy looked down at Bet for a moment, as though hovering on the edge of something he couldn't quite say. "It does."

"They've waited a long time for it," Malcolm said. "That can make one appreciate it more."

Jessica ran up and flung her arms round Bet's knees. "Dollies?"

"Of course." Bet scooped Jessica up and carried her over to where the children were gathered.

"She's very kind to the children," Malcolm said.

"She loves them." Sandy watched Bet drop down on the hearthrug surrounded by the children. He was smiling, but he'd seemed abstracted all day. Malcolm wondered if it was the tension of being in society with Bet. He hadn't seen anyone look askance at them. "I'm glad you both came," he said. "It means a great deal to O'Roarke and Laura."

"We wouldn't have missed it." Sandy turned to Malcolm with sudden decision. "Look here, Malcolm. O'Roarke's your father."

"Yes," Malcolm said, unsure where the conversation was going. "We don't make any secret about that."

"Have you always known? Even when you were a boy?"

"No. That is—" Malcolm thought back to moments playing catch, fishing, poring over books. Falling asleep with a steady hand stroking his hair, knowing a sense of security that had been rare in his life. "Looking back, I think a part of me always knew. But I didn't consciously admit it to myself until a few years ago. And I didn't ask O'Roarke until a year and a half ago."

Sandy nodded, brows drawn. "Did you know your father—that is, Alistair Rannoch—that he wasn't—"

"Wasn't my father at all? I think I always suspected that as well. I was fairly certain of it before I was in my teens."

"Was it hard? I mean, knowing—"

"Alistair and I never had a father-son relationship. Inheriting all this"—Malcolm waved a hand encompassing the grandeur of the Berkeley Square house filled with Alistair's art treasures —"from a man who wasn't my father at all? That's hard, at times. Of course, as my wife would be quick to remind me, I don't believe in inherited privilege, which means it shouldn't matter. And perhaps that I should reject my inheritance. Which of course I haven't been able to bring myself to do."

"I'd never suggest that." Sandy's frown deepened. "Do you think —is that what a fellow should in honor do?"

"I tend to agree with Shakespeare that honor is but a word. And a word that's all too often an excuse for bad behavior. Challenging to reject an inheritance in the world we live in today. Not even very feasible, legally."

"Yes, but if one could. If one is living a lie—"

"Sandy?" Malcolm studied his young friend. "I fear I'm a bit slow. I should have realized something started these questions now."

Sandy drew a breath. "I think a part of me has suspected for a bit. Like you. Like other fellows, I suppose. William Lamb. Billy Dunstable. Pater always treated me very decently. If he seemed to favor Matt a bit, it made sense because Matt was the eldest. Never thought it meant more than that. Or at least never admitted that it might. Always knew my parents weren't madly in love, but then one doesn't expect one's parents to be. Doesn't like to think of them that way, as I said when you came to ask me about Aunt Anne. But with Matt gone—It's as though a curtain my parents have always kept over themselves was pulled down. Or perhaps I see them differently because Matt's gone. I can't quite be sure. Father took to spending more time at White's than usual. Mama wouldn't talk about Matt, but I knew she was crying. Not a surprise. Might have felt like crying myself if I weren't so angry at Matt. Then, one night, I'd come to dine with them and I heard Mama saying 'I'm so sorry, he's your heir.' And Papa said, 'He's still my heir.' And Mama said, 'But if he can't come back—.' And Papa said, 'We've got Sandy.' Which, if I'm right, was very decent of him. And then Mama said, 'But he's not—.' And somehow I knew she was going to say, 'your son,' even though she broke off. And Father said, 'What's done is done. That's been true since he was born.' They broke off then. I ducked into the water closet because I couldn't face them. By the time I went into the drawing room, Father was reading the paper and Mama was embroidering and we talked about my cousin's new baby and all sorts of trivialities. Just like we've been doing since Matt had to leave. It wasn't until I got home that I could properly think about it. I almost told Bet, but I couldn't bring myself to. Couldn't put it into words. But the more I thought about it, the more sense it made."

"Sandy—" Malcolm struggled for the right words, as he did when one of his children asked a question he couldn't answer easily (which was more and more of their questions these days). "You don't know anything for a certainty. Your instincts may well be right. But even if they are, it takes more than biology to make someone a parent. Your father obviously decided he was your father when you were born, if not before. Which is a great deal more than Alistair Rannoch did for me."

"Yes, but if he's not—"

"Who's to say what makes a father?" Malcolm was keenly aware of his own son, though he didn't let his gaze shift in Colin's direction. "He raised you. He loves you."

"I feel like a fraud."

"You're yourself, Sandy. You'll always be, no matter what facts you uncover. A loyal friend. A devoted lover to Bet. A thoughtful son to your parents."

"I can't help but wonder—I can't possibly ask my mother. I don't think I could in any case, but after what's happened to Matt I know for a certainty I can't add to her strain. But—did you wonder? Who your real father was? Before you knew about O'Roarke for a certainty?"

"Sometimes. And then I'd tell myself it didn't matter."

"Did you really believe that?"

Again, he tried to force himself to honesty. "It matters that it's O'Roarke. But that's because I already had a relationship with him. He already was my father to all intents and purposes. If it had been someone I'd never met or barely knew, who'd never taken an interest in me—I'd be curious, I think. It's human nature to be. But I'm not sure it would really matter."

Sandy nodded. "I wish I could do the same. I'm not sure I can. I want to tell Bet."

"I think you should."

"Really? You don't think it's a betrayal of my mother?"

Malcolm glanced at Bet. She had Jessica and Drusilla in her lap and was bent over them, laughing. "I think your secret—your mother's secret—would be safer with Bet than with anyone."

Sandy looked at Bet as well, and gave a sudden grin. "I think you're right."

CHAPTER 16

"*H*ave I mentioned that you're wonderful friends?" Laura said. "Truly, it couldn't have been lovelier. I'm sorry I ever said anything about not wanting a wedding celebration."

Mélanie smiled at her friend. Evening shadows filled the Berkeley Square library. The leafy plane trees were dark smudges in the square garden, fading into the darkening sky. The wedding breakfast guests were long since gone. So were Laura's family, Manon and Crispin and their children, Paul and Juliette and their children, Allie, Geoff, and Claudia, and Rupert, Bertrand, Gabrielle, Nick, and Stephen, who had stayed on for dinner. Malcolm and Mélanie, Laura and Raoul, and the two Davenport couples were gathered in the library over whisky and tea while the children played at the far end.

Raoul had an odd smile on his face. He had been smiling all day, which was unlike him, unlike even the much-changed man he had become. "Moments like this should be shared with people one cares about. It's good to be reminded of that." He hesitated a moment. "And it was good, beyond words, to share it with all of you." He moved to Laura's side and put a hand on her shoulder.

Laura turned her head and pressed her lips against his fingers.

"I'm glad Lord Weston came to the wedding," Mélanie said. "It was good to see him looking happy."

"Yes." Raoul smiled. "He told me he's taking Lady Darlington driving tomorrow. From a man with Weston's reticence, that's practically a declaration." He drew Laura's hand up to his lips. "And I'll own my own happiness makes me particular happy to have had any role in helping someone else reach for theirs."

"It's good to savor victories," Archie said. "We've actually had quite a few lately."

Emily came running up from the midst of the children's game. "Am I Colin's aunt?" She looked from Laura to Raoul and then at Mélanie and Malcolm. "Or his sister? Or his cousin?"

Laura and Raoul looked at each other and then exchanged glances with Malcolm and Mélanie. "What an excellent question," Raoul said. "Sometimes we're different things to the same person."

"I think you can decide what you want to be to Colin," Malcolm said.

"Maybe not the same thing all the time," Mélanie added.

"You can talk to Colin about it too," Laura said.

Emily considered. "I think I'll just be his aunt when I need him to do what I want."

"That sounds like an excellent plan," Malcolm said.

Emily nodded and ran back to the other children, where she appeared to be informing Colin of her newfound authority.

"Well done," Archie murmured.

"I'd swear you all had that planned," Cordelia said.

"Making it up as we go along." Laura gave a rueful smile.

"I think you handled it admirably." Frances shifted Philip, who was nursing. Despite her words, there was a faint line between her brows. She had been rather quiet all evening, Mélanie realized. Mélanie had put it down to Frances's not wanting to take center stage from Raoul and Laura, but now she wondered if there was more to it.

"Fanny?" Raoul dropped down on the arm of the sofa, holding Laura's hand. "Is something wrong?"

"How could anything be wrong today?" Philip had fallen asleep in her arms. She shifted him to Archie and took Francesca from her husband. "But I had a rather odd conversation with Amelia Carfax. I hesitated to bring it up today, but I don't know that I can hesitate any longer."

"We're neither of us under any illusions that our wedding stops the other intrigues we're in the midst of," Laura said.

Frances looked down at the baby in her arms and drew a breath. "It concerns Alistair," she said. And then went on to tell them.

Mélanie felt tension shoot through Malcolm's arm, which was wrapped round her shoulders. "Good God," he said.

"It's certainly a surprise," Mélanie said.

"Yes," Malcolm said. "But in some ways, not as much as it might have been. Only this afternoon, Sandy told me he's come to suspect Marchmain isn't his biological father. Apparently he overheard his parents talking after Matt's exile."

"Does he suspect Alistair Rannoch is his father?" Cordelia asked.

"I'm quite sure he doesn't. He told me because he knows Alistair isn't my father. That Raoul is. He—wanted to know how long I'd known. And how I felt about it." He looked at Raoul. "I told him it was easier because you've always been my father in so many ways."

"At least we can stop wondering if Sandy had a role in the intriguing around his getting the junior secretaryship," Laura said.

"It definitely offers an explanation of whom Lady Marchmain gave the Craanford information to," Raoul said.

"So that's why the League want Sandy to have the junior secretaryship?" Cordelia asked.

"Out of loyalty to Alistair?" Archie frowned. "It's possible. I wouldn't say the League are driven by friendship much of the

es have a number of League members who are
?y may have simply wanted to put his son in
...ion. Or perhaps they thought they could tell
...u at some point and that it would give them a hold
...un or ensure his loyalty."

"If Lady Marchmain told Cresswell about Anne Darlington's letters, she may still be actively connected to the League," Laura suggested. "Perhaps they did it as a favor to her. Perhaps in response to something else they wanted her to do."

"Interesting thought," Raoul said. "If she's the source of the Craanford information, she does seem to have been very enterprising as an agent."

"And her elder son went to work for the League," Archie said. "Perhaps not as unwittingly as we thought."

"All of which suggests we may be in the midst of something that isn't yet resolved," Malcolm said, "however well we've managed to extricate Weston and Lady Darlington." He took a sip of whisky. "Alistair is a Scottish form of Alexander. Not that that should have told us anything. Both are common enough names. But Lady Marchmain seems to have wanted to link Sandy to Alistair in some way." He frowned across the room. "Given the life Alistair lived, I shouldn't be surprised he sired children. Very likely there are more I don't know about. I suppose I've always known that, but since Alistair wasn't my father—" He shook his head.

"Children aren't responsible for their parents," Raoul said in a quiet voice. "You certainly aren't responsible for Alistair."

"No, I never thought I was. But now I know—" Malcolm stared at the glass-fronted bookcase.

"It's difficult to keep it to yourself." Harry, as usual, didn't shy from putting difficult choices into words.

"You've said you're glad you know," Raoul said in a quiet voice.

Malcolm met his father's gaze. "Of course I am. But I found out my father was someone I knew. Someone I care about. Loved.

Who had actually been a father to me. And I already knew Alistair wasn't my father. If my biological father had been someone I'd never met, I'm not sure how much the truth would have mattered to me. I said that to Sandy earlier today, in fact."

"I don't think it would matter to me," Harry said. "I had little enough relationship with my own biological father. At least, I assume he was my biological father."

"He was," Archie said. "You look like him. For that matter, you look like me."

"And I'm rather glad you're my uncle by blood. But if I suddenly found out someone else had fathered me, at this point, I don't think I'd care very much. It doesn't change who I am."

"I had a strained enough relationship with my own father," Raoul said. Malcolm looked at him in surprise. So did Mélanie. Raoul almost never talked about his parents. "I've maintained my whole life that birth doesn't define one. I still maintain it. But it would have meant—it would still mean—something to me to learn he wasn't my father. It would have been even more dramatic when I was Sandy's age. I'm not sure, to be honest, whether it would have made my life better or worse."

"Gisèle wanted to know," Mélanie said.

Malcolm turned his glass in his hand. "So she did."

"And she seems to have handled it quite well," Raoul said. "At least on the surface."

"She always knew Alistair wasn't her father," Frances said.

Malcolm looked at her.

"No," she said, "I didn't know about Sandy. I didn't know about Lady Marchmain and Alistair. As Amelia said, Alistair might have been particularly determined to keep the truth from me. As to how Sandy may react—I'd say it probably has to do with how he feels about his father. That is, Lord Marchmain."

"He's fond of him in a rather distant way, I think," Malcolm said. "But hearing Alistair sired him or not hearing it doesn't change the fact that Marchmain isn't his biological father." He took another drink of whisky. "He was obviously wondering about it today. And he needs to be put on his guard against the League. I need to tell him."

FRANCES LOOKED UP AT MALCOLM. THEY WERE ALONE IN THE library as she settled Francesca in her basket. Everyone else had moved into the hall. "You've never asked me," she said.

"No," Malcolm agreed. "I never felt I had any right to. I still don't."

Frances folded her arms over her chest. "My children haven't asked either. Which is rather surprising."

"Perhaps it means they're comfortable with who they are." Malcolm touched her shoulder.

"You have to have wondered."

"What was between Alistair and you is your business. And Alistair's, I suppose, when he was alive."

"And you wonder if I'm sure myself?" She raised a brow. "It's true in some cases it's a close enough thing I can't be completely sure. But I'm fairly sure he was Aline's father. And Chloe's."

Malcolm was silent for a moment. "I had wondered. Allie has his eyes. Though it rather proves Raoul's point about none of us being defined by our birth. Allie and Chloe are both extraordinarily nice people."

"Yes, far more so than their mother."

"I was about to say they have their mother's innate kindness."

"Don't talk twaddle, my dear."

He was silent for a moment. "Edgar—"

"Yes, they're Edgar's half-sisters. As well as his cousins."

"And Sandy Trenor's half-sisters as well."

"That's why I told you." Frances tucked the blanket about her infant daughter. "Too many secrets are tumbling into the open."

CHAPTER 17

S andy stared at Malcolm. "So we're—"
"Friends. As you already know, Alistair wasn't my father."

"No, of course not. I'm not thinking."

"I'd be proud to have you for a brother, Sandy."

"He wasn't a very nice person, was he? Alistair Rannoch. My —father."

"No. I'm a bit biased because we never got on, but he certainly wasn't kind. And you needn't call him your father if you don't wish to. He didn't raise you. Lord Marchmain did."

"If it comes to that, a passel of nurses and governesses and tutors did most of the work. But Pater—Marchmain—was very decent to me, despite his suspicions. Christ, do you think he knows? About Alistair Rannoch?"

"I don't know. It's not—"

"Unusual in my parents' set. Our parents' set. Yes, I know that. Just never thought until a few weeks ago that I—"

Bet, who was sitting beside Sandy on the sofa in his sitting room, slid her hand into Sandy's own. "I love you, Sandy. You're you."

Sandy smiled down at her, like a man seeing his way through a fog. Then he looked back at Malcolm. "So this Elsinore League. Alistair Rannoch started it?"

"With others. But it was largely his. Yes."

"It makes me feel responsible."

"He didn't make himself responsible for you. And even if he'd raised you, his sins aren't on your head."

"No, but I can't but feel—you're trying to bring them down."

"To check them, at least."

"I want to help. Look, Rannoch, I know I'm not a spy, but there must be something I can do."

It was very like what Malcolm's brother-in-law Andrew had said to him four months ago when Gisèle had decided to stay undercover. "There's plenty for all of us to do," Malcolm said.

"Including me," Bet said.

"That's good of you," Malcolm said.

"We're not saying it to be good." Sandy regarded him for a moment. "How much does my mother know?"

Malcolm returned his young friend's gaze. "I don't know."

"But she gave Alistair Rannoch information twenty years ago?"

"She seems to have done. If she was in love with him, that could account for it."

"Matt worked for them."

"For Lord Beverston. We didn't think he knew about the League."

"*Didn't.*"

"This does complicate things," Malcolm admitted.

Sandy gave him a look that was somehow at once vulnerable and hardened with growing adulthood. "It doesn't change my wanting to help. I won't tell her. I don't expect you to believe me—"

"I trust you, Sandy. More than I trust most people. But it's hard for any of us to know what we'd do in all situations. I can't even be certain about myself."

"Fair enough. Control what information you give me. But let me help."

"SO WE HAVE MORE ALLIES," MÉLANIE SAID.

Malcolm nodded. They were on one of the black metal benches in the Berkeley Square garden, beneath the shade of a plane tree, watching the children enjoy a game of tag while Berowne dozed in the sun. "Sandy has a good head on his shoulders. I hate that he's in the middle of this, but I think he actually can be of help. As can Bet. And it's not a bad thing for Sandy to come to terms with the world's complexities. For him or for Bet."

Mélanie slid her hand into her husband's own, picturing Sandy and Bet at the wedding the previous day. From the look she caught in Bet's eyes watching Sandy in unguarded moments, Mélanie was sure Bet was all too well aware of the world's complexities. And of what they meant for her own and Sandy's future.

"Don't underestimate Sandy," Malcolm said, as though he read her thoughts. "Even if he is Alistair's son. Perhaps especially because he is Alistair's son. Alistair was a lot of things, but he certainly was brilliant and an astute judge of people. Though Sandy has a sensitivity Alistair quite lacked."

Mélanie studied her husband. A breeze rustled through the tree branches and cast shifting shadows over Malcolm's face. To the outside world, Alistair Rannoch was his father, and by his own account there was a time he himself hadn't been sure. For all he might claim to be relieved Alistair wasn't his parent, what did it mean to him that Alistair's illegitimate son was such a focus of the League to this day, whereas Alistair had displayed no interest in Malcolm himself? "I know this doesn't make Sandy your brother," she said, choosing her words carefully. Sometimes, the better one knew someone, the more difficult it was to speak, because one knew just what traps one was stepping round.

"But it's a tie between us. I'm not sorry for that. Well done, Jessica," Malcolm called, as their daughter tagged Colin. He looked back at Mélanie. "Oh, did you mean am I bothered that Alistair and the League seem more interested in Sandy than they ever were in me? On the contrary. I couldn't be more relieved not to be a focus of the League's interest."

Mélanie tightened her fingers round Malcolm's own. "I wouldn't entirely say you weren't. They set Laura to spy on us. I don't think even the League do that with that many people."

"No." Malcolm's gaze settled for a moment on Laura's daughter, titian plaits flapping in the breeze as she ran after Colin. "But I actually prefer that to being the subject of their scheming." His brows drew together. "The League haven't shown much interest in Edgar. Which I suppose isn't surprising, as Alistair never showed much interest in him."

Even now, Mélanie didn't fully understand Malcolm's relationship with his brother save that they were no longer as close as they had once been. She sensed Malcolm himself wasn't sure why they had drifted apart. "You're wondering if you should tell Edgar about Sandy?" she asked.

"I think I'm going to have to, the next time he's back from France. And warn him about the League. Just because they haven't targeted him doesn't mean they won't. Alistair's legacy is difficult to contend with." Malcolm turned his head as Laura and Raoul emerged from the Berkeley Square house, and lifted his hand in a wave. "For any number of reasons, I'm very glad O'Roarke is my father."

EPILOGUE

One month later

The night Malcolm was born he'd paced the floor of his London hotel. Frances, only fifteen, had sent him updates, and at last the news that he and Bella had a son. Relief that Bella and the baby were all right had washed over him in a deluge. He couldn't say how long he'd stood staring down at the paper, but it had been minutes together before it fully dawned on him that he was a father.

It had been two days before he'd seen Malcolm. Fanny had smuggled him into Bella's house, and Fanny had put Malcolm in his arms. He could still remember the weight of his infant son, so insubstantial, yet heavy with responsibility. A responsibility he could well be said not to have lived up to.

But that night, all the awareness of parenthood had been there, trembling along his nerve endings. A joy and fear that he had had to keep bottled up inside, because the truth of Malcolm's parentage had to remain secret.

He hadn't known the precise night Colin was born. Not until

after the fact. He'd known he'd abrogated the right to more than the interest of a friend long before Colin's birth. But he'd been keenly aware of the timeframe, concerned about what might be happening. Relieved, as he had been at the news of Malcolm's birth, when Mélanie sent him a brief note that the baby had been born and they were both well. Relieved, but aware he had no claim to either the joy or fear of new parenthood.

This was different. It wasn't waiting for news of a mission, it was taking part in the mission. Albeit in a very limited way, the sort of role that left one feeling helpless while a comrade ran unthinkable risks. Save that he couldn't remember a mission where he'd been anything like as unable to offer practical aid as he was now.

Laura's fingers tightened round his own. "Talk nonsense. Anything. I could drown in trivialities."

"You look beautiful."

"That *is* nonsense."

"No." He pushed the sweat-dampened hair off her forehead and kissed her temple.

Laura's hand tightened round his own. He slid his arm round her until the spasm ended.

"Splendid," Geoffrey Blackwell said. "Shouldn't be long now."

Mélanie put a glass of chipped ice in his hand. "Give her a piece at a time. It can help."

Laura looked past him at Mélanie. "When you did this the second time you could remember the first. I wonder if that makes it easier or harder?" She took a piece of ice, then gasped as another contraction hit.

"Capital," Blackwell said. "I can see the head. You can start pushing, Laura."

Raoul slid his arm beneath his wife's shoulders. Laura looked up at him and for a moment he'd swear what he saw in her gaze shot straight through to his soul.

It was a blur after that. Laura's muscles straining beneath his arm, her fingers clenching his hand, deep breaths, and then suddenly a small cry, and a small, squirming human on Laura's chest.

"Sweetheart." Laura's fingers curved round the baby's head.

Raoul touched the child's small hand and kissed Laura's hair. It was some moments later before he realized they had a daughter.

MALCOLM LOOKED UP AT THE OPENING OF THE STUDY DOOR, AWARE his fingers were not quite steady. Mélanie leaned against the doorjamb. She was smiling. "You have a little sister. Laura's well."

Malcolm released a breath he hadn't known he was holding. "How's O'Roarke?"

"He looks a bit green, but he managed very well. Almost as well as you. He's waking the children up. Do you want to come meet your sister?"

MALCOLM FOLLOWED MÉLANIE TO LAURA AND RAOUL'S ROOM TO see Emily sitting in the bed, holding her baby sister in her arms, between her mother and Raoul, who was perched on the edge. Colin was curled up at the foot of the bed holding onto Jessica, who was studying the baby with wide eyes. "Baby."

It had been Jessica's first word, and babies continued to intrigue her.

"Just so." Raoul smiled at her.

"What are you going to call her?" Colin asked.

Raoul raised a brow at Laura. Laura looked between him and Emily. "Clara?"

"That's pretty," Emily said.

"Clara." Raoul curved his fingers round his daughter's head.

Malcolm watched them for a moment, then walked to the bed and stroked a finger along his little sister's knuckles as he once had with Colin and Jessica. Clara's small hand closed round his finger. Malcolm smiled down at her. "Welcome to the family, little one."

HISTORICAL NOTES

The events of the United Irish Uprising were very real, but the Craanford incident, Algernon Weston, Anne Somercote Darlington, and their letters are entirely fictional. The actual Chancellor of the Duchy of Lancaster in 1819 was Charles Bathurst.

THE GLENISTER PAPERS

**Malcolm and Mélanie Suzanne Rannoch's adventures in espionage and investigation continue in Tracy Grant's new historical mystery.
On sale May, 2019.**

*London,
September, 1819*

"Remind me again what we're doing here?" Malcolm Rannoch murmured, casting a glance round the ballroom.

Mélanie curled her gloved fingers round his arm. "You need Sir Winston for your anti-enclosure bill."

Malcolm looked down into his wife's sea-green eyes. "And we were going to stop playing these games."

"We can't entirely stop playing them."

Malcolm glanced at Laura and Raoul O'Roarke. "And somehow you got pulled into it."

"There are a number of Spaniards here," Raoul said.

"And James and Hetty," Laura said.

"Besides it was an excuse to order a new gown," Mélanie said.

"Oh, well." Malcolm smiled at his wife. "Why didn't you say so to begin with? Such a charming gown certainly deserves an outing."

"Confess it, Malcolm. You didn't realize it was new until just now."

Malcolm took in the silver gauze over azure satin. "But I did notice you were looking particularly lovely."

"The perfect answer." Laura looked at Raoul. "I hope you're taking notes."

"He'd have noticed it was a new gown," Malcolm said. "O'Roarke's attention to detail is flawless."

"Laura's is new too," Mélanie said.

"Of course it is," Raoul said. "And stunning."

"Liar." Laura smiled at her husband.

"I'm not lying about your being stunning."

"Heavens, only a few months, and I seem to have forgot how crowded Mayfair ballrooms get." Cordelia Davenport joined them, her arm linked through her husband Harry's.

"Let me guess," Malcolm said. "You have a new gown."

"How very perceptive of you, Malcolm." Cordelia smiled at him. "Harry didn't notice."

"Deduction. I didn't notice Mel's or Laura's, but it finally occurred to me the three of you went shopping together."

"One would almost think you were a spy," Harry said. "But then I'd never think you all bought new gowns simply to intrigue your husbands. If so you'd know you have no need of gowns to do so."

"You're brilliant, Harry." Mélanie smiled at him.

Harry stopped a waiter and procured glasses of champagne to hand round. "Remind me why we're here. Besides the gowns."

"Politics," Mélanie said.

"Spain," Raoul said.

"Family," Laura said.

"And tracking the League," Malcolm added. "If—"

He broke off, because a flash a movement across the room caught his eye, an echo of memory that sent him spinning back eight years, before the rich gold of the hair and the swirling green of the gown registered. Candlelight shimmered off damask wall-hangings and gilded paint. Champagne glasses clinked. Voices pinged off the coffered ceiling. The sights and sounds he had known all his life, here and abroad. People he had known all his life were all round him. And for a moment, like a trick of theatrical illusion, it was all gone and he was rooted to the ground, staring across the ballroom at a ghost.

"Darling?" His wife's familiar voice cut the stillness.

"Sorry. Someone I haven't seen for a long time. I had no notion she was back in London."

Raoul and Laura had gone completely still. Mélanie's gaze was a little questioning. He'd seen their friends in similar situations. He should warn Mélanie. But how to do it so quickly? He and Mel had always been quick to communicate, but this was something he scarcely even had the language for.

He met her gaze for a moment and saw a glimmering of understanding flash in her eyes. And then it was too late, because his ghost was no longer across the room but standing before them.

"Mr. Rannoch. It's been a long time."

"Mrs. Ashford. I had no notion you were in Britain."

"We've only just arrived from the Argentine."

"May I present my wife Mélanie?" The familiar social ritual came to his rescue like lines from a well-rehearsed play. "Darling, Katelina Ashford. I knew her in Lisbon, but she and her husband left for the Argentine before I met you."

"Mrs. Ashford." Mélanie's smile was faultless.

"Mrs. Rannoch." So was Kitty's.

"I believe you met Colonel Davenport in Lisbon," Malcolm said. "Though not Lady Cordelia. And of course you know O'Roarke," he added, wondering just how much Raoul knew about

Kitty and her activities, and Malcolm's own involvement with her. "But I don't believe you've met his wife, Laura."

Kitty shook hands with Laura and Cordelia. Was it his imagination, Malcolm wondered, that their interaction was subtly different from the same one between Kitty and Mélanie?

"I heard Malcolm had married," Kitty said. "I didn't realize you had as well, Mr. O'Roarke. My felicitations."

"Thank you. It was very recent," Raoul said.

"A number of things have changed for all of us. But then I imagine the end of the war shifted things for everyone. Especially those of you who remained in Britain. We felt very far from things in Argentina, though we did get news from home, of course." Kitty smiled at Mélanie. "I was so pleased to hear Malcolm had found happiness. Your brilliance is talked of even in South America."

"You're very kind, Mrs. Ashford, though I know exaggeration is part of the language of diplomacy." Mélanie said.

"But not among friends. I confess it is quite a relief to meet old friends from the Peninsula."

"Are you in Britain long?" Malcolm asked.

"I'm not quite sure yet," Kitty said. "I decided to bring my children back to Europe rather suddenly. My husband died nine months ago."

At this point, her being a widow could hardly matter. Not to him. Not except that it might give Kit a chance for a happier life. But the news still hit him like a shock of rainwater.

"I'm sorry," Malcolm said, also using the language of diplomacy. "My condolences."

"Thank you." Kitty's voice was steady, her gaze composed. However she may have changed, she hadn't lost her ability to dissimulate. "It was a shock. Though when one is married to a soldier, one is always prepared to some degree."

"I'm very so sorry," Laura said. "My father is a former soldier. And my late husband was one as well, though he didn't die in battle. Much as one knows the risks I don't think one is ever quite prepared for it."

Laura almost never talked about her first husband. Malcolm had the oddest sense she was attempting to come to everyone's conversational rescue.

"We saw so many of our friends fall in the Peninsula and at Waterloo." Mélanie's voice was warm with sympathy. Malcolm thought only he would have caught the slight tremor that ran through her. "It's such a difficult life being a soldier's wife. I'm so very sorry. It must be particularly hard for your children."

"Yes," Kitty said, "though they are also a great comfort. I'm sure having been married to Malcolm for almost seven years you aren't a stranger to fearing for your husband. Lady Cordelia can't be. I imagine Mrs O'Roarke isn't either though she's been married for a shorter time."

"I would almost say the fears are commonplace," Laura said. "Except that they never could be."

"I greatly relieved when Harry sold out," Cordelia said.

"I confess I was terrified for Malcolm, particularly at Waterloo, for all he wasn't a soldier," Mélanie said.

"Malcolm always ran his own risks," Kitty said.

"Not so much anymore." Malcolm pressed Mélanie's arm closer to his side.

Kitty gave a lopsided smile that had the familiarity of a favorite book suddenly falling open to a wellborn page. "But then you never would admit to them, would you?"

"If you mean I always avoided exaggeration, then you are perfectly correct."

"My point precisely. I imagine Mrs. Rannoch is quite familiar with your habit of understatement."

"Perfectly." Mélanie smiled at Kitty.

"Whereas Mr. O'Roarke never made a secret of the dangers he ran," Kitty said. "Merely the details of those dangers."

"My work is much less dangerous these days," Raoul said.

"Which doesn't mean not dangerous." Laura smiled up at him with ironic affection. "All things are relative."

"Or perhaps the dangers we all face are simply different these days," Kitty said.

"Well put, Mrs. Ashford," Harry said.

"You must call on us while you are in London, Mrs Ashford," Mélanie said. "And bring your children. Our son and daughter would love to meet them. The O'Roarkes and their daughters live with us as well, and the Davenports and their daughters are frequently at our house."

"That would be delightful. Oh, I see my late husband's godmother beckoning to me from across the room. Do pray excuse me. I look forward to talking later."

Kitty was gone in a swirl of silk and diamonds, leaving silence in her wake.

"I hadn't heard about Ashford." Harry stepped into the conversational void with his usual acuity. "But we were in different regiments. I didn't know him well."

Malcolm also hadn't known Harry all that well at that time. There was no reason Harry should know about Malcolm's relationship with Kitty. None except that he was Harry.

"I had no notion she was back," Malcolm said, aware of the need to fill the void with something approaching normality. He glanced at Raoul. "Did you?"

"No," Raoul said in a low voice that gave little away. "Like you I hadn't even heard Ashford had died."

And there was no particular reason Raoul should know. None except that he was Raoul.

"Has she ever been to England before?" Laura asked.

"I don't think so," Malcolm said. "She married Ashford in the Peninsula."

"Rannoch." Henry Brougham clapped Malcolm on the shoulder. "Thank you for being here. Or perhaps I should thank Mélanie." He shot a smile at her. "Come with me. Sir Winston is in the card room and he's just won a hand so he's in an agreeable mood. Forgive us, Mélanie. Lady Cordelia. Mrs. O'Roarke. Davenport. O'Roarke."

"Of course." Mélanie gave a smile from her days as a political wife. "It's why we're here after all."

～

Mélanie watched her husband cross the ballroom with Henry Brougham. Without turning her head, she was aware of Katelina Ashford on the other side of the room. Funny. She'd always known there must be a woman like this. No, not like this. The woman had remained tantalizingly out of focus in all her imaginings. But she'd always known he must have former lovers. He might not have her level of experience, but he was no novice in the bedchamber. And knowing Malcolm, whatever his romantic past, it involved not transitory relationships but women he'd cared about. Meeting Katelina Ashford she'd known it was more than that. This woman wasn't just a former lover but a former love.

They both had pasts. It shouldn't bother her. But seeing Malcolm's past cross a ballroom to them couldn't but bring her up short. More than it should have done.

Cordelia slipped an arm through Mélanie's own. Harry, Raoul, and Laura had been claimed by others. Perhaps, Mélanie thought, deliberately so, so she and Cordy could talk. "That was splendidly done," Cordelia said.

"I don't feel very splendid."

"I don't think it's ever easy. No matter how prepared one is."

"I hardly have any right to be upset."

"Rights have nothing to do with it, dearest. I don't need to remind you that Malcolm's besotted with you, do I?"

"Malcolm's never been besotted with anyone." At least not

since she'd known him. What had he been like when he first met Katelina Ashford?

"You know what I mean. The past can't disrupt what's in his eyes when he looks at you. Even if he doesn't notice your new gown."

Mélanie laughed. "Malcolm only notices gowns when they're disguises. And I know perfectly well what we have."

"Well then."

Which didn't make her questions go away. Malcolm had left the room with Brougham. But she had a very shrewd notion of where would go after they spoke with Sir Winston. And with whom.

After he and Brougham concluded their talk with Sir Winston, Malcolm made his way to the library without consciously deciding to do so. The room was empty, a brace of candles lit on the mantel and another on the library table. He stood for a moment, drinking in the scents of ink and leather, his mind filled with past echoes from another library in a time when he had been another person. A few moments later he heard the door open. Eight years and he recognized her footsteps. Though she was wearing a different perfume. Camelias, not jasmine, and an echo of spice.

"I thought I'd find you here." It was the low, husky voice with an undercurrent of amusement from all those years ago. Far less contained than her voice in the ballroom.

He turned and surveyed her. "I'm not to be found in the library at parties as inevitably as I once was. But it seemed the best place for us to talk." Her hair was cropped shorter round her face than he remembered and it had streaks of gold that hadn't been there before. The Argentine sun perhaps. The lines round her mouth and eyes were a touch deeper, lending even more of a touch of sardonic mockery. But the eyes themselves were as brilliant and questioning as ever and her mouth twisted which just the same irony. "It's good to see you, Kit. You look well."

"So you do." She paused for a moment. "I thought you might still be angry."

"If I am, it's only with myself. Surely you realized that."

"I hope so. That is, I hoped you'd been able to move beyond it."

"I don't know that I'll ever move beyond it. I don't know that I'll ever want to. But at times I find I'm happy to remember."

"Thank you. That means a great deal." She drew a breath that seemed as fragile as the delicate green glass beads round her throat. "Marriage seems to agree with you." She hesitated a fraction of a second, fingers taut on the ivory and emerald silk of her fan. "Your wife is very lovely."

"My wife is a remarkable woman in a number of ways. Her beauty is the least of it." What in God's name could he say about Mélanie without either betraying too much or not giving her enough credit? "I'm beyond fortunate."

"And you're a father."

"Yes, we have two children. Colin and Jessica."

"I'm glad." Her voice caught for just the fraction of a second, like a boot toe scraped over rock. "I always thought you'd make a good father. When I knew you, you seemed determined to deny yourself all that."

He didn't owe her an explanation. Or perhaps, given the past, he did. "I met Mélanie during the war. It seems an insult to say she was in want of protection, but in the eyes of the world she was. Otherwise I doubt I'd ever have risked offering for her. I didn't think I'd make the best husband."

Kitty tilted her head to one side, a faint smile in her eyes that brought a tug of memory. There was a time when that smile had driven rational thought from his brain. "You always tended to underrate yourself, Malcolm."

"Or to see myself clearly."

She shook her head. "The same Malcolm." She hesitated a moment. Her gaze moved over his face with that clear-sighted look he knew so well. "You seem happy."

"I am." Simple words. Words he'd once hesitated to use. Words he once thought described a past that was a mirage. But that now were as real as anything in his life.

"I'm glad."

"I hope—"

"That I am?" She shrugged, a familiar, elegant gesture. "I've always been able to manage. The last few months have been particularly challenging. But you know what my marriage was."

"I'm sorry. If I'd known I'd have written—"

"To offer condolences?" She gave one of the ironic smiles that were so uniquely hers. "You've never been a hypocrite, Malcolm. I don't deny I felt badly, but mostly out of guilt that I didn't mourn Edward more. And even then I had enough self-respect to recognize that he didn't deserve a great deal of guilt."

"Thank God for that."

She smiled again, with more sweetness. "But I've found compensations. I have three children now. I enjoy them. Losing Edward was harder because they lost their father. But they are a great comfort."

"It means a lot, being a parent." For a moment his voice was thick as cotton wool.

"Yes."

They regarded each other, the past hanging between them. Unventured waters, unexplored possibilities, things they would never know.

"I thought of my children most when my husband died," Kitty said. "He was proud of them, but as you can imagine he wasn't the most attentive father. They miss him, of course. At least the elder two do. I'm afraid the baby doesn't even remember him. But it's not the wrench it would be for some children. They're part of why I wanted to come back here. To have my children grow up closer to where I did. Though I confess Britain seems quite alien even after spending so much time in British diplomatic circles."

"It can be a difficult place to adjust to," Malcolm said. "I'm still getting used to it again after our time in Italy. I think Mel still feels like an outsider at times. Though I think she'd also tell you it gets better."

"You've gone into Parliament," Kitty said, her voice a shade huskier than before.

"Surprised?"

"When I knew you, you claimed you'd never go back to Britain. And that you'd lost your taste for politics. But even then you were far more of an idealist than I was. As I learned to my sorrow. Our sorrow, perhaps."

Malcolm braced his arms on the chairback behind him, legs crossed at the ankle. "We saw the world differently. Most people do, to a degree. Even friends. Even lovers. Even husbands and wives."

Kitty raised a brow. "Your wife lost her family in the Revolution, didn't she? I imagine that might give you somewhat different perspectives. But if you mean you and your wife disagree, you seem to have got past it. I'm not sure you and I ever would have done."

"We'll never know."

"And never face disillusionment. We faced enough as it is." She regarded him for a long moment. That look had maddened him, the look that implied she saw things he could not. Especially as he had to admit she was often right. "I'm glad you're in Parliament. You always had too much integrity for the spy game."

"Integrity can be difficult to hold on to in Parliament as well."

"And I don't imagine you've been able to leave off being an agent completely. One never can."

"I've done my best."

"Are you saying Carfax is willing to let you go?"

"Carfax has learned there are limits to what he can ask of me."

"I'm impressed." Kitty fingered a fold of her gown. "Your wife investigates with you. When I heard that, I couldn't but wonder—"

"Yes, she was an agent as well." Amazing how often the truth served, even when one was implying quite the opposite.

"That would help, I would think. To give you common ground."

"We grew close working together." Again the truth. Though this time it cut a bit close to the truth of his relationship with Kitty.

"Perhaps the only way a spy can fall in love."

"Perhaps the closest a spy can come to trusting."

Kitty moved into the room. The candlelight warmed her skin and sparked off the gold in her hair. "I think about you often," she said. "I'll confess I miss you at times. But I've always thought it's a good thing things never went further between us. Seeing you now, happily married, settled in your world, I'm even more convinced of it. It's not easy, living in exile."

He'd done just that with Mélanie and been quite happy, despite the challenges. But that had been Mel. Hard to imagine having that sort of relationship with anyone else, even Kitty, who had once meant so much to him. And impossible to tell Kitty, however he had once trusted her, that he and his wife had run from Britain because Mélanie might be arrested for treason. Even though Kitty had been an agent herself. Perhaps especially because she had been an agent herself.

"All relationships have challenges. One never knows what they can endure until one faces it. Sometimes they come out stronger."

"And sometimes they're smashed to bits. I never wanted that for us."

"I'll never stop—"

"My dear Malcolm, you were always too inclined to feel guilty. We both made choices. You have nothing to reproach yourself with. For what it's worth, I wouldn't give up the memories for anything." She watched him a moment longer. "She doesn't know, does she? About us."

"No. I'd hardly—It wasn't wholly my story to share. And—"

"I wasn't here for you to ask. Whatever you want to tell her now, you have my blessing."

"Thank you. Knowing Mel, she's already guessed a great deal. Though she'd also never ask for an explanation."

Kitty ran her fingers over her fan. "It sounds so easy to leave the past in the past. But then that never quite works, does it?"

"Not entirely. One tries to find things one is happy to remember."

"Which can be a challenge. With a spouse. Or a current lover."

"Mel knows what we have. As to the rest of the past, we're all adjusting to the end of the war. Trying to make sense of where we were left standing when the music stopped playing, as O'Roarke says."

"I was surprised to see him tonight. Not so much to see him— he's always had a habit of popping up in unexpected places— but to learn he's married. I thought—"

"He and his first wife divorced."

Kitty tilted her head to one side. "You're on even closer term than I remembered."

Malcolm smiled. "I forget how long it's been. A number of things have changed. I've learned a number of things. O'Roarke's my father."

"Good God." Kitty drew a rare breath of surprise. "I'm sorry, I didn't mean—I knew he was a friend of your family—"

"Yes. I know I told you I wasn't on the best terms with Alistair. I don't think I ever came out and said I was quite sure he wasn't my father. I suspected O'Roarke was for some time. Perhaps even when I knew you, though I don't think I'd quite come out and admitted it to myself. It was quite a relief to learn Alistair wasn't my father and someone I actually liked—someone I was already close to—was."

"I'm glad it's been so easy." The faintest of questions lingered in her voice. "Thank you for trusting me with the information."

"It's a fairly open secret these days. The children know. O'Roarke lives with us. At least he does when he's not fomenting revolutions abroad. Laura was a good friend of ours before she and O'Roarke met. She has a daughter from her first marriage, and she and Raoul have just had a little girl."

"It all sounds positively domestic." Kitty adjusted one of the silk roses on her bodice. "I was a bit surprised to find you so domestic. I'm even more so to hear Raoul O'Roarke is."

"As Laura said it's all relative. He's hardly settled down."

"I imagine not given the situation in Spain."

"Quite." Malcolm kept his voice easy. Given Kitty's actions in Spain during the war and Raoul's and what Kitty knew and didn't know about Raoul's, this was fraught ground. "I don't think he could avoid being involved. But he spends more and more time in Britain. He's been here since his and Laura's baby was born."

"Convenient."

Was it his imagination or was there just the faintest undertone to Kitty's words? He was jumping at shadows. Probably inevitable when so many spectres emerged from his past.

Malcolm watched her, remembering the quick calculation that could take place behind those brilliant eyes and that sardonic smile. "Out with it. Kit. What are you really doing here?"

She smoothed the links of her bracelet. "Who says I'm doing anything here but what I said?"

"I just did." Malcolm folded his arms across his chest. "You were always adept at seeing through me. But I'm rather good at doing the same where you're concerned."

She looked up at him, her head tilted to one side. "The same Malcolm. I never could lie to you."

"On the contrary. You did it very well on several occasions." He kept his gaze steady on her face. "What are you doing here, Kit?"

She hesitated.

"I don't need to be an agent to guess it's to with the situation in Spain."

Kitty released her breath and gave a sudden smile. "I should know it's a fool's errand to try to keep anything from you. And in truth I meant to tell you. I was trying to work out how. There was a lot in the Argentine to keep me busy. It's a new country now. Exciting to have been part of it. But I've kept in touch with people in Spain."

"With Victor, I imagine. It's all right, I've seen him once or twice. We can meet with civility."

"My cousin has a good mind, but he's not free of annoying ideas about defining a woman's honor. But yes, he's kept me apprised of the situation in Spain. Told me I was well out of it when Ferdinand repudiated the constitution and restored the Inquisition."

"And now he's working with the rebels."

"As you might expect."

"You've come back to work with them. But you said you need help. You have a specific mission?"

"We're trying to build support. I have a list of people who aren't committed to either side to try to win over." She hesitated.

"A good strategy. But you said you were going to tell me. You need help? Help I can give?"

Kitty drew a breath. "I assume you've heard of the Goshawk."

"What is it about birds and agent's code names? Yes, of course I heard of the Goshawk during the war. A brilliant agent who carried out raids on French patrols, supplied guerrillero bands with intelligence, and surprised starving villages with gold and bread. As much myth as reality, I always thought, though I heard enough stories from people I trusted to believe there was some truth behind the myth. But I haven't heard anything of the Goshawk since before Waterloo."

"Imagine if he emerged now. In a country on the verge of revolt."

"He's one man. The country already has plenty of reasons to revolt."

Kitty tilted her head to the side. "Dear Malcolm. You always tended to overlook the power of the power of symbols. Perhaps not surprising in one with your lack of religion. But I would think your training as an historian would at least give you an intellectual appreciation of what symbols can do."

"It's taught me that symbols tend to exist on the surface with other forces driving change beneath."

"Perhaps. They can still be a potent rallying cry. Not to mention that the Goshawk's network would be invaluable if we could resurrect it."

Malcolm folded his arms over his chest. "Are you saying you know who he is? Or she?"

Kitty's brows knotted together. "Are you saying it's a woman?"

"I don't know who the Goshawk is. But the accounts are vague enough it's a possibility. Do you know?"

"If I knew my mission would be much easier."

"Victor wants you to find him. Or her."

"Symbol or not, he—or she—could rally a number of people. And bring invaluable expertise to the fight."

"And you think the Goshawk is in Britain?"

"I think I may be able to pick up his trail here.

I have it from a reliable source that one of the Goshawk's former associates is in London."

"A number of people who fought in the Peninsula are in London."

"I have a name. Marianne Larimer."

Malcolm drew a breath, picturing the decorous woman he had last seen sipping tea in Berkeley Square. "She's a soldier's widow."

"For shame, Malcolm. I'm a soldier's widow."

"You know what I mean, Kit. She's not an agent."

"That you know of."

"Are you saying you do know she's one?"

Kitty ran the strap of her reticule through her fingers. "My source wasn't entirely clear. But if she knew the Goshawk I'd suspect she was. You didn't know every British agent in the Peninsula, Malcolm."

"No, of course not. And I'm not claiming I did. But I knew the Larimers fairly well. I liaisoned with John on some missions. I'd have thought I'd heard or noticed something." Though he hadn't with his own wife.

"It's possible John didn't know, at least not all of it. Edward didn't know a lot about me. In any case, I need to talk to her, and it's precisely because you knew them that I need you. I scarcely knew Marianne Larimer, and you know I was never entirely accepted in British society. I imagine it's difficult for your wife as well, for all I've heard her described as the toast of the beau monde."

"Yes. It's been difficult."

"Well then. The Goshawk is a secret, a secret she's kept for over half a decade. She won't tell me."

"And you think she'll tell me?"

"You can get people to talk, Malcolm. You've always had a genius for it. And she trusts you."

"And you want me to play on that trust."

"That's what agents do, Malcolm. You have more scruples than most agents, but you're still an agent. Don't try to fob me off with stories about 'former.'"

"Believe me, even I recognize those stories for folly now."

"Well then." Kitty tilted her head to one side. "However divided we may have been eight years ago, we're on the same side in this, Malcolm. I can't believe you don't want Spain to change. You must be sick about what it's become. What the British helped it become."

"What we helped them help it become me."

Kitty didn't flinch from his gaze. "Yes, all right. We didn't get the Spain I thought I was fighting for. And there may have been a kernel—perhaps rather more than a kernel—of truth to your claims all those years ago."

He found himself smiling, though not without irony. "You'll still say anything to win, won't you, Kit?"

"That isn't why I said it. Or at least, it's not all of why I said it."

"Honest as always."

"Except on occasion."

Malcolm pushed himself away from the chair. "You're right. I'm sick about what Spain's become. If I wasn't a father, I might be there myself right now. I can't guarantee I can get Marianne to talk to you. But I'll go with you to see her."

"Thank you."

"There's no need for thanks. It's simple enough, and as you say, we're aligned in this."

"It will be awkward with you wife."

"On the contrary. She'll only be sorry she doesn't have a connection to Marianne herself. O'Roarke and Laura will help too if they can. And the Davenports." It all sounded very convenient. Except for the fact that Kit didn't know she and Raoul had been working for opposite sides.

"You've none of you left off being agents, have you? You and Raoul and Harry Davenport. And you've drawn your wives into it as well."

"We all undertake investigations from time to time."

"Yes, even in Argentina I heard stories. It seems your wife is very adept at them as well."

"It's something we learned we could share early in our marriage." Another truth that sidestepped Mel's role as an agent.

"She won't mind your going to see Mrs. Larimer with me?"

"Why should she? Mel trusts me."

Kitty watched him for a moment. "Trust is a wonderful thing in a marriage."

ALSO BY TRACY GRANT

Traditional Regencies

WIDOW'S GAMBIT

FRIVOLOUS PRETENCE

THE COURTING OF PHILIPPA

Lescaut Quartet

DARK ANGEL

SHORES OF DESIRE

SHADOWS OF THE HEART

RIGHTFULLY HIS

The Rannoch Fraser Mysteries

HIS SPANISH BRIDE

LONDON INTERLUDE

VIENNA WALTZ

IMPERIAL SCANDAL

THE PARIS AFFAIR

THE PARIS PLOT

BENEATH A SILENT MOON

THE BERKELEY SQUARE AFFAIR

THE MAYFAIR AFFAIR

INCIDENT IN BERKELEY SQUARE

LONDON GAMBIT

MISSION FOR A QUEEN

ABOUT THE AUTHOR

Tracy Grant studied British history at Stanford University and received the Firestone Award for Excellence in Research for her honors thesis on shifting conceptions of honor in late-fifteenth-century England. She lives in the San Francisco Bay Area with her young daughter and three cats. In addition to writing, Tracy works for the Merola Opera Program, a professional training program for opera singers, pianists, and stage directors. Her real life heroine is her daughter Mélanie, who is very cooperative about Mummy's writing time. She is currently at work on her next book chronicling the adventures of Malcolm and Mélanie Rannoch. Visit her on the Web at www.tracygrant.org

© Raphael Coffey Photography